Fallen Ridge

RJ DERBY

RJ Derby

Fallen Ridge

Copyright © 2024 by RJ Derby.

No part of this publication may be reproduced, distributed, or transmitted in any form or by any means, including photocopying, recording, or other electronic or mechanical methods, without the prior written permission of the publisher, except as permitted under the *Australian Copyright Act 1968*. For permission requests, contact the publisher/author.

The story, all names, characters, and incidents portrayed in this production are fictitious. No identification with actual persons (living or deceased), places, buildings, and products is intended or should be inferred.

Book and Cover design by *Caged Mad Artwork*

ISBN: 978-1-7637941-0-8

First Edition: November 2024

10 9 8 7 6 5 4 3 2 1

For Krystle

PROLOGUE

FALLEN RIDGE IS A TOWN with secrets. It lies nestled in a valley, hidden by mountains looming as silent sentries. Its name alone is enough to make travellers think twice before venturing near. Once, they said, Fallen Ridge had been a lively place—a town built on dreams, on the promise of endless prosperity. But that was before the mine collapsed and buried thirty men alive. Before the river turned black and thick as tar, killing all that dared to drink from it. Before the last light left the eyes of its townsfolk, one by one.

Now, *the Ridge* is a hollow place, the remnants of a decayed past clinging to the present. Those who live here bear its weight, shouldering secrets that linger in their bones, twisting them into shadows of the people they might have been. The Ridge holds them fast, a spider capturing its prey, and no one ever truly leaves.

Daisy Miller has a face that doesn't seem to belong to her life. With soft curls framing her porcelain skin, she could pass for a classic beauty queen. But beneath Daisy's beauty lies a coldness that chills to the marrow. She works the register at the town's lone grocery store, her eyes flat and emotionless as she rings up boxes of cereal and tins of soup, day in and day out. Some say she never blinks. Others swear she wears the perfume of rotting flowers. Only her mother knows why Daisy keeps her windows open at night and whispers to the shadows in her room, begging them to stay away.

It is the guilt, of course. Everyone in the Ridge knows Daisy drowned her baby boy. She'd been seventeen, desperate, with no one to help her, and when the baby wouldn't stop crying, wouldn't let her sleep, something inside her had snapped. She'd held his tiny head under the water in the kitchen sink until his screams bubbled into silence. But what most didn't know was that Daisy could still hear his cries echoing in her mind every time she closed her eyes. She could feel his tiny fingers clutching at her in the night, his weight pulling her deeper into the darkness. The townsfolk might whisper, might judge, but none of them truly know what it's like to carry a ghost that small and fierce.

Then there's Sheriff Tom Dalton, a hulking man with hands big as shovels and eyes of flint. He walks the streets of The Ridge with a swagger, his silver badge gleaming under the dim lights of the streetlamps. He's been sheriff for as long as anyone can remember, and his rule is ironclad. If you need something kept quiet, you go to Sheriff Dalton, and he makes it disappear– for a price. But no one dares ask him about his brother, about the screams that echoed from his basement when he was a boy, or why his mother disappeared so suddenly one sultry July night.

People in Fallen Ridge have theories. Some say Tom fed his brother to the wild dogs that prowled the edges of town; others believe he did worse. But when the sheriff's mother vanished, no one asked questions. She'd been a haunted woman herself, her face carved with fear, and the town had known she wouldn't be missed. Tom is a fixture now, a symbol of Fallen Ridge itself—powerful, haunted, and hiding something dark. And if his brother's ghost haunts him, whispering from the shadows of his past, no one would ever know.

In The Ridge, everyone has a secret, and Pastor Lou Bennett is no different. The town looks to him as a beacon of light, of salvation, but even the pastor carries a darkness in his heart. He leads his flock every Sunday, preaching repentance and forgiveness, his voice smooth as honey, rich as wine. Yet there's a reason no one dares look too closely into Pastor Lou's past, a reason why his wife disappeared without a trace one stormy autumn night.

Rumours ripple through town that the pastor buried her beneath the church itself, sealed her into the stone walls, her mouth open in a silent scream, her hands outstretched, reaching for freedom that would never come. They say that when he preaches, he can feel her there, cold and accusing, trapped just inches from freedom, her bones twisted and broken, her fingers brushing the bricks, clawing for escape. But Pastor Lou wears his smile like a mask, his sermons laced with sweetness and redemption, and the townsfolk look to him with reverence, never questioning the darkness that looms just beneath the surface.

And then there's the widow Margaret Larkin, who lives on the edge of town in a crumbling Victorian house that seems ready to collapse in on itself at any moment. Margaret is as old as the hills, her face a map of lines and creases, her eyes sharp, missing nothing. She's lost three husbands, each one dying under "mysterious circumstances," as the townsfolk whisper. They say Margaret is a witch, that she's put a curse on the town, that the mine collapse, the poisoned river – all of it – can be traced back to her.

But what they don't know is that Margaret is cursed herself. Each night, she can see her husbands' faces in the mirrors of her house, feel their breath on her neck as she lies in bed, hear their voices calling to her from beyond the grave, begging her to join them. Margaret has tried everything to rid herself of their spirits – rituals, sacrifices, burning sage until her lungs ache from the smoke – but they remain, bound to her, watching her every move, their eyes burning with hatred. And Margaret, proud and bitter as she is, refuses to give them the satisfaction of her fear.

The people of Fallen Ridge keep to themselves, going about their lives, but the weight of their secrets thickens the air, stifling and inescapable. At night, the town is silent, the streets empty save for the occasional stray cat or the creak of a weathered sign swinging in the wind. But if you listen closely – if you dare – you can hear the whispers, faint and mournful, the voices of those long gone, calling out from the shadows.

They say that if you stay in Fallen Ridge long enough, the town takes a piece of you. It slips into your mind, crawls into your heart, whispers in your ear until you find yourself bound to it, just like everyone else. You start carrying secrets, small at first, but they grow, taking root in your soul. And no matter how hard you try to leave, no matter how far you run, The Ridge is always with you. It becomes part of you, a darkness inescapable.

And so they stay. Daisy at the register, her hands trembling as she rings up another bottle of milk, the ghost of her child clawing at her from the shadows. Sheriff Dalton, his brother's voice calling to him from the depths of his mind, driving him deeper into silence. Pastor Lou, his sermons hiding the guilt that presses down on him, the walls of his church echoing with the whispered curses of his dead wife. And Margaret, old and defiant, staring into the mirror as the faces of her husbands' glare back at her, waiting for her to finally give in.

In Fallen Ridge, the past never truly dies. It lingers, festers, and feeds on the souls of the living, and those who call it home know that one day, they, too, will join the voices in the shadows. They will become part of the town's secrets, bound to it forever, just as it was always meant to be.

Welcome to Fallen Ridge. And be careful what you hide.

Chapter One

ICY RENT

It was always the same for Mark. Just as a storm brings grey skies, or the taste of iron signals fear. No matter what he did, the images were there – burned into the inside of his skull, a brand of red-hot, smoking memory. Two years had crawled by, sluggish and unyielding, and still, he couldn't shake them. No, they danced behind his eyes, shadows cast by the flicker of candlelight. Ghostly. Taunting.

Nancy.

Every night, when the world outside was quiet, and the darkness settled in, a heavy, wet shroud, Mark found himself staring up at the ceiling, his eyes tracing the spiderweb cracks, crawling and spreading with each sleepless hour. The cracks spread across the ceiling, veins in an ancient corpse, branching out, reaching, maybe even for him. It had become a ritual. That's what he told himself. A ritual. Just like brushing his teeth or saying his prayers. Lying there, a corpse in its box, he waited for sleep that wouldn't come until the hours were so small they felt like seconds. And every single night, it was the same.

Nancy's face would be there – floating above him, her eyes doll-like in their emptiness, her smile twisted, mocking him. Her voice, that sweet, sing-song voice that had a way of pulling him in, a hook that caught him at his core, whispered to him from the darkness. Her presence was so clear he could feel the warmth of her breath on his skin, smell the lavender perfume she always wore – cheap and sweet and suffocating. It had been two years since she'd left him, and yet she was still here. She was everywhere.

"Mark," she'd whisper, her voice just a slither, a damp kiss on the air. "You never were enough." And then she'd laugh, her laughter, a tinkling, brittle sound of breaking glass.

He hated her. *God*, he hated her. Hated her for haunting him, for drilling into his mind, a rusty screw twisting deeper and deeper until he couldn't tell if it was his heart or his head that was bleeding. And she danced, always danced – just like she had on their honeymoon when the world felt soft and warm and real. But now, those memories twisted into nightmares, her movements jerky, a marionette with tangled strings. Dreams and reality bled into one another, creating a fog where time moved slow and cruel, a blade dragging through skin.

Most nights, he just watched. It was easier that way. Let her dance, let her sway, let her torment him until he was empty, a husk lying on sweat-damp sheets. The first light of dawn would claw its way through the curtains, an acid burn on his eyes, and only then would he drift off into a sleep that felt like a blackout – nothingness. *God, give me nothing*, he'd think, praying to any god who might still be listening.

But the days – oh, the days were even worse. Sunlight hit him, too bright, too harsh, peeling back his skin. When he opened his eyes, the images of Nancy would disappear, as if afraid of the light, but the emptiness they left behind gnawed at him.

Tonight, though, the daylight was still hours away. The night was thick, the kind of blackness that felt alive. Mark threw the covers off in a fit of rage, kicking them into a tangled heap on the floor. He swung his legs out of the bed, and the icy touch of the floorboards sent a jolt up his spine.

"Cold," he muttered, clenching his fists. "Why does *everything* have to be so *goddamn* cold?"

Nancy had once been warmth, like the sun on your skin after a long winter. Those lips of hers – back then, they were hot embers. When she kissed him, he could feel the burn, the heat that promised something more. And later, when things had cooled down, her kisses were still a comfort, the cool side of the pillow after a long day. But those days were gone. Her lips, when they kissed him at the end, were cold. Ice cold.

Icy Rent, he thought, the phrase popping into his head like a virus he couldn't shake. He'd only been renting her, hadn't he? *Borrowing*. And in the end, she belonged to someone else. Someone better. Someone who could make her scream a name that wasn't his.

He stood up; the floorboards creaking underfoot, and made his way down to the kitchen. The house felt like a tomb, and the shadows reached out for him, curling around his ankles. Light was unnecessary; he knew the house by heart. He'd walked it a thousand times, night after night, through the thick darkness and heavy silence.

Grabbing his cigarettes and lighter from the table, he pushed open the back door and stepped into the chill. The wind was sharp, biting into him, raising goosebumps along his arms. It was a ritual now – just another part of the long, lonely nights. He fumbled with the pack, pulled out a cigarette, and lit it. The flame flickered, fighting against the wind. He took a deep drag, feeling the smoke burn down his throat, hot and satisfying.

He turned his eyes up to the sky. The stars were barely there, a shroud of mist wrapping around the world in a death grip. Everything felt distant. The cold seeped into his bones; it was better than lying in the stillness, that empty pillow beside him, mocking.

Two years. Two *goddamn* years, and he felt dead already. As if the light inside him had been snuffed out, the candle flame killed by a careless hand. As he looked out into the backyard, his eyes fell on the small mound near the fence, barely visible in the darkness.

Nancy had left him for another man. And this was a man Mark couldn't fight. He knew that now. He knew he'd lost. But it wasn't to just any man. It was to him. To the one no one could win against.

She'd called his name – called it as she died, blood leaking from her lips. The last word she spoke, that whisper that came out, a sigh… "Jesus."

Mark's knuckles whitened as he gripped the railing. "I let you go," he said, his voice low, almost a growl. "You went to him, and you think you won?" He spat the words into the night, his breath visible in the cold air. "Well, guess what? I'm still here, and you're just dirt now."

But he knew, even as he said it, that it was a lie. *She'd* won. She'd always win. Because no matter how many times he smoked his way through the darkness, no matter how many cigarettes he burned to ashes, she was still there. She would always be there. And every night, he'd find himself standing over that mound, whispering into the cold.

He whispered it again, the name that had taken everything from him.

"Jesus."

The icy hand of winter gripped his heart as he stared at the dirt beneath him. The sky opened, and a shroud of mist fell, covering the ground. Mark stood there, letting the cold sink into his bones. He knew he'd never feel warm again.

Chapter Two

THE LEFT HAND OF GOD

P ASTOR LOU BENNETT HAD always how to make people believe. His words enfolded them as if in a warm embrace, offering comfort and reassurance, each syllable infused with a conviction that made his congregation feel as if they were walking a little closer to God. The Ridge was the kind of town that needed hope. The people lived in the shadow of old sins, surrounded by ghosts they couldn't escape. And Pastor Lou was their salvation, a light in their darkness.

But before he was Pastor Lou, he had been just Lou Bennett – no collar, no congregation, no burden of faith to wear like armour. Back then, he had been young, his heart filled with fire, and when he met Alice, it was as if he'd found the missing piece of his soul. She was like no one he'd ever met – free-spirited, sharp-witted, with a laugh that sliced cleanly through the deepest silence. They were married within months, a whirlwind romance that took everyone by surprise.

Yet, just as quickly, the fire between them had turned to smoke, drifting into dark places they could not escape.

The church became Lou's refuge. As Alice grew colder, more distant, he found himself drawn to the sanctuary of God, seeking a peace he could not find at home. He started preaching unofficially, sharing his thoughts on faith with anyone who would listen, filling the church with words that felt like an escape from the emptiness that had grown between him and Alice.

But Alice hated the church. She hated the time he spent there, the way he gazed at the pulpit, as though it was a wellspring of life's deepest answers, the way he seemed to slip away from her, inch by inch. She would stand in the back, her arms crossed, watching him with a cold, silent disdain that burned hotter than any argument.

Their fights grew louder, uglier, each word a jagged edge that cut deeper into the wounds they'd both tried to ignore. She accused him of hiding behind his sermons, of using God as an excuse to avoid facing their problems. He accused her of bitterness, of jealousy, of pulling him into the darkness she wore as heavily as a mourner's veil.

Then, one night, it had all come to a head.

It was late autumn, the air thick with the smell of rotting leaves, the sky a blanket of storm clouds that hung low and heavy. Lou had just finished a late-night service, the kind of intense, impromptu sermon he gave when he felt the weight of his own sins pressing down on him. The church was empty, save for the flickering candlelight and the echo of his own voice ringing in his ears.

As he closed the door behind him, he saw her there, standing in the shadows, her face half-hidden in the dim light, her gaze fixed on him with an intensity that sent a shiver down his spine.

"Lou," she said, her voice low, edged with something he couldn't quite place. "We need to talk."

He didn't respond, his mind racing with the words he hadn't yet said, the accusations he hadn't yet made. He'd spent months burying his resentment, his anger, trying to find forgiveness in the pages of scripture, but in that moment, he felt it all come rushing to the surface.

"Not *here*, Alice," he said, his voice tight, his gaze fixed on the ground. "Not in the church."

She laughed, a hollow, bitter sound that slashed through the silence. "Oh, *now* you care about the church?" she sneered, her eyes narrowing as she took a step closer. "*Now* you care about where we argue? You spend every waking moment in this place, hiding from me, hiding from yourself—"

He clenched his fists; the words bubbling up inside him, sharp and vicious, fuelled by months of silence, of unresolved tension. "Maybe I wouldn't have to hide if you weren't so *hell-bent* on dragging me down with *you*!" he snapped, his voice rising, each word slipping out like poison.

For a moment, she was silent, her gaze fixed on him, her expression unreadable. Slowly, she took a step back, her hands trembling, her face pale.

"You're a *coward*, Lou," she whispered, her voice filled with a sorrow so deep it seemed to cleave his heart. "You hide behind your sermons, behind your faith, but you're just as lost as the rest of us. And one day, you'll have to face that."

She turned to leave, her footsteps echoing through the empty church, each step a reminder of the widening gulf of darkness that stretched between them. Lou watched her go, his heart pounding, his mind racing with anger, with resentment, with a dread he could not name.

And then, without thinking, he followed her.

The storm was fierce that night. The sky lit up with flashes of lightning, the air thick with rain. Lou followed Alice through the winding streets, his mind reeling with anger, regret, and a desperation he could not name.

They stopped outside the church, the air filled with the sound of rain pounding against the ground, the wind whipping through the trees, filling the air with a low, mournful howl.

She turned to face him, her gaze fixed on him, her expression filled with a sorrow he could not understand.

"Lou," she whispered, her voice trembling, each word slipping out like a confession, a plea. "I don't want to be alone."

He felt his anger melt away, replaced by a hollow, aching sorrow, a sense of loss so profound it felt like his very soul was being torn apart. He reached out, his hand trembling, his gaze fixed on her, his heart pounding with a dread he could not name.

But as his hand brushed her shoulder, a bolt of lightning lit up the sky, illuminating her face, and in that moment, he saw her as she truly was – broken, hollow, a shadow of the woman he had loved.

He let his hand fall, his gaze fixed on the ground, his heart heavy with the weight of his own sins.

"I can't help you, Alice," he whispered, his voice barely more than a breath. "I'm sorry."

And with that, he turned and walked away, his footsteps echoing through the empty streets, each step a reminder of the darkness he had left behind.

The next morning, Alice was gone.

He searched for her, his heart pounding, his mind reeling with fear and regret, but there was no sign of her, only the faint scent of lavender that lingered in the air, a haunting reminder of the woman he had lost.

He told the townsfolk she had left, that she had gone to stay with her sister up north. But in his heart, he knew the truth. Alice was gone, lost to him forever, a ghost that would haunt him until the end of his days.

And in time, the whispers began.

The townsfolk spoke of a woman's ghost, trapped within the walls of the church, her mouth open in a silent scream, her hands outstretched as though reaching for freedom that would never come. They said that when Lou preached, he could feel her there, cold and accusing, her bones twisted and broken, her fingers brushing against the bricks, a ghost trapped within the stone.

But Pastor Lou wore his smile like a mask, his sermons rich with sweetness and redemption, his words as smooth as honey. He buried the weight of his sins beneath layers of charm and scripture, filling the church with words of forgiveness, of salvation, each syllable slipping from his lips like a prayer, a desperate attempt to find peace in the darkness.

At night, however, when the church was empty, and the pews were shrouded in shadows, he could feel her there, her presence pressing down on him, filling him with a dread so deep it seemed to swallow him whole.

The scratching began two years after she disappeared.

It started as a faint, barely audible noise, a soft, rhythmic sound that drifted through the church, filling the air with a chill that seeped into his bones. At first, he thought it was the wind, the old building settling, a trick of his own guilty mind. But as the days went by, the sound grew louder, more insistent, a constant, desperate scratching that filled the church, echoing through the silence like a haunting melody.

He tried to ignore it, tried to drown it out with his sermons, his prayers, his desperate pleas for forgiveness. But the scratching followed him, a constant reminder of the darkness he had buried, the sins he could not escape.

One night, unable to bear it any longer, he stayed late after his sermon, the church empty, the air thick with silence. He sat in the front pew, his Bible open before him, his hands trembling as he whispered prayers into the darkness, his voice barely more than a breath.

"Please," he whispered, his voice filled with desperation, with fear. "Please, forgive me."

But the scratching continued, relentless. Each scrape of her fingers against the stone was a reminder of the darkness he carried, the sins he could not escape.

And then, in the silence, he heard it – a faint, pitiful whisper, soft and broken, drifting through the air like a ghostly sigh.

"Lou..."

His breath caught in his throat, his heart pounding, his mind reeling with fear and disbelief. It couldn't be real. It was his mind, his guilt, his sins come back to haunt him. But as he listened, the whisper grew louder, more desperate, each word seeping into his mind like a slow, spreading venom, leaving him with a dread so heavy it felt like sinking.

"Lou..." the voice whispered again, filled with a sorrow so deep it seemed to pierce through him like a knife. "Please... let me out..."

He stumbled back, his hands trembling, his heart racing as he stared at the wall where the sound came from, his mind reeling with fear, with guilt, with a despair so deep it seemed to swallow him whole.

And in that moment, he knew the truth.

Alice was there, trapped within the walls, her soul bound to the church, bound to him; a ghost that would haunt him until the end of time.

And as he fled the church, the scratching echoing through the silence; he understood he would never be free. She was his punishment, his penance, a haunting reminder of the darkness he had buried within himself, a ghost that would haunt him until the end of time.

Chapter Three
IT ALL ENDS IN TIME

PAUL SAWYER WAS A man of habits, some good, most not so much, but who wasn't a creature of repetition? If he'd picked up a few quirks along the way – a penchant for profiling, a restless inner monologue, and an itch for cigarettes every now and again – then he considered himself only a little worse off than anyone else in their forties. He was standing at the far end of a cavernous living room, staring out the warped and yellowing windows that seemed to peer back at him with the grim knowledge of ages. A strange, hollow chill had settled into his bones almost immediately.

"Haunted," Mabel Hunter whispered. She was supposed to be showing him the property, but she looked as uneasy as someone attending their own trial. "Bad *mojo*," she added in a tone as soft as a prayer.

Sawyer didn't move. He tapped his notepad—an old leather-bound notebook he used for jotting down observations that would later sound even more ridiculous when he read them back to himself. He didn't believe in half of what he did, but paranormal investigation paid well enough to get by. A thin, weary smile played on his face as he glanced back at Mabel.

"Not mojo, Mrs. Hunter," he said, leaning a little too far into his charm, aiming to see her squirm. "We'd call it paranormal activity."

"Oh, *paranormal*, huh?" she said, her tone one of forced politeness, her arms wrapped around herself like armour against an unwelcome chill. She looked every inch the church-going widow, and he could tell Mabel didn't have the slightest idea what he was talking about.

Paul sighed and returned his notebook to his coat pocket, feeling the weight of years of scribbled notes pressing against his chest. He'd been in this business for five years now – too many, if he was honest. He'd seen his share of haunted houses, witnessed shadows and cold spots and many eerie nonsenses. But in the end, he mostly just wanted the pay-check and maybe a drink at the bar to wash it all from his mind. Maybe it was time to hang up the paranormal gig, finally retire from this endless carousel of creaks and cold drafts and inexplicable noises in the walls.

He was only forty-one, after all. Maybe a switch to private investigations was overdue. Private work came with danger too, but not the kind that snaked its way into your mind, tainted your dreams, and left you feeling as though you were fraying, thread by thread.

"Mr. Sawyer?" Mabel's voice snapped him back to reality. She was staring at him with that all-too-familiar, slightly horrified expression people got when they realised they'd wandered into a house that didn't feel empty, not even when it was. He nodded at her, encouraging her to speak.

"It's, uh, chilly in here," she muttered, eyes darting up to the ceiling as though expecting something to drop, something wet, something —

blood.

The word sliced through his mind like a scalpel carving into flesh. He pulled his gaze from her, fixing instead on a door he hadn't noticed until that very moment, a door small and strange, standing like a secret waiting to be let out.

"Mrs. Hunter," he asked, his voice sounding foreign, almost hollow, "where does this door lead?"

She looked up at it, her lips tightening. "I don't know, Mr. Sawyer. But the previous owners—the Matthews—told me it was always... *scratching*. Every night, they'd hear it, faint at first, but then..." Her voice trailed off, leaving an unpleasant silence between them. She stared hard at the door as if daring it to do something.

"Scratching, huh?" He arched an eyebrow and stepped closer, feeling an uncomfortable pressure settle on his shoulders. His gaze travelled over the doorframe, noting the faint streaks of paint-covered silicone, the six screws lined up along each edge, and a hasty patch of plywood covering what must have once been the door handle. He reached out a hand, feeling a cold sweat prick at the back of his neck.

Somewhere in the depths of his mind, a voice bubbled up like a drowned body breaking the surface of a dark lake.

Kill her, Sawyer. Go on, do it, just open the door, let us out, just you, me, and the rat who wants to see you bleed.

He jerked his hand back, recoiling as though he'd been burned. Mabel was watching him now, concern etched deep into her wrinkled face.

"Mr. Sawyer? Are you... alright?"

He forced a smile, though his skin felt hot and tight. "I'm fine, Mrs. Hunter," he muttered, wiping a hand across his brow. It came away damp.

He stared at the small, mocking door that seemed to invite him closer, daring him to touch it, open it, let whatever was on the other side loose. His mind was throbbing with thoughts that weren't his own, vile things that tasted like rust and smoke, and he wanted nothing more than to leave, to get the hell out of this house, this room.

"Did the Matthews ever say if they'd heard any voices?" he asked, his voice barely louder than a whisper. He wondered if she'd noticed the strain in it.

She nodded slowly, her gaze faraway. "They... they mentioned something once. They said it wasn't a *voice* they could hear with their ears, exactly. More like a voice *inside* them, whispering things... *awful* things. Things they'd never think on their own." Her voice dropped to a whisper. "Things like killing each other."

The words made Sawyer's stomach churn. He was familiar with darkness – he'd been a forensic officer, after all, had seen the worst sides of humanity laid bare in pools of blood and gore. But this was different, darker, something that left fingerprints on your soul rather than just your skin.

"Maybe it's best I run my tests alone," he said. He wanted to sound polite, to clarify that her presence wasn't necessary, but his words came out sharp-edged, almost a command.

She hesitated. "Mr. Sawyer, I don't know what happened in this house, but... well, promise me you'll be careful. *Please?*"

The earnestness in her voice, that fragile hope that maybe he'd understand, washed over him. He gave her a brief nod. "I promise."

And then she was gone, slipping out the front door with one last backward glance, the look on her face almost mournful. He heard the front door lock behind her, the metallic click sounding as final as the seal of a tomb.

The silence that settled was thick, pressing in on him from all sides. He stood in the centre of the room, staring at the tiny door, and he felt a familiar shiver run up his spine, the one his mother used to call "*a goose walking over your grave.*"

He stepped closer, his heart pounding a slow, heavy rhythm in his chest, and he could feel it – something from the other side, breathing in the darkness just behind that plywood patch, waiting.

Sawyer wasn't a superstitious man, but in that moment, he felt like a man staring into the maw of something old and patient, something that had been there long before him and would be there long after he was gone. He reached out a trembling hand toward the door, his fingers brushing the rough wood, and he felt the cold bite of metal as his fingers found the head of one of the screws.

Sawyer, we're waiting. Just one turn and it will all be over. Sawyer, one twist, one pull, and we'll be together.

The voice was louder now, clearer, almost familiar. Sawyer pulled his hand away, stumbling back, his heart hammering against his ribs. He wanted to laugh, to scream, to run, to do anything but stand there staring at the door that watched him with a dark, knowing patience. He turned away, forcing himself to step back, to look anywhere but at that tiny, mocking portal.

Paul wouldn't touch it. Not today, never. But he knew, deep down, that the house wasn't done with him yet.

In the driveway, Mabel Hunter was gone, the house standing silent, watching. And somewhere inside, the scratches began anew, soft and faint, like the whisper of a memory just waiting for someone – *anyone* – to hear them.

FALLEN RIDGE

Sawyer barely registered the click of the front door, the fading footsteps of Mabel Hunter, or the soft rumble of her car's engine as she disappeared down the drive. Already, he was focused on the screws of the little door, paint curling away under the edge of his knife. Each twist of the Swiss Army blade peeled back secrets that had long settled into silence.

Oh yes, Sawyer, tic-tac-toe, let's open and go...

The words in his head jabbed like a schoolyard bully, cruel and relentless, bouncing around with the strange cadence of a nursery rhyme gone sour. He gritted his teeth, pressing back against the invasive taunt, trying to drown it out with sheer concentration.

"*Shut up,*" he muttered, barely aware he'd spoken aloud.

But the voice only laughed, a sound that prickled the skin at the base of his spine. His heart thrummed with excitement, each twist of the screws sending a thrill up his arm, as if each one was unlocking something long buried, something terrible. *What if*, a part of him whispered, *this was what you've been searching for all along?* Something bigger, darker than any haunt he'd dragged from the shadows. Hadn't he left his old job for this strange calling precisely because of that need? Maybe this... this was what he'd needed all along.

Twisting that last screw brought a certain, unsettling pleasure. He felt it loosen, then fall with a dull thud onto the hardwood. Each screw that clattered to the floor left him feeling somehow lighter, stronger, his breathing heavier in the still air. It was almost like being a kid again, he thought, remembering the first time he'd felt real fear – looking down at his mother's pale, lifeless face, her mouth twisted in an expression of eternal surprise, as if death had taken her unawares. He'd never forgotten that feeling: the sense of something final, something that didn't yield answers.

And now, that feeling was back, alive in his chest as he pried open the door with the edge of his knife, feeling the wood give under pressure. The door creaked, reluctant and stiff, as if it didn't want to open, as if the house itself was holding it shut. But with a grunt, he pushed harder, forcing the door wide enough to peer through, his breath misting in the sudden, sour draft that rolled out to greet him.

Come on, Sawyer... step into the dark, come to where the shadows bark...

The stench was thick – a cloying smell of rot, time, and something else, something acrid and burnt. He held his breath, nose wrinkling, his mind reeling as he leaned closer, straining to see past the threshold. Only darkness lay beyond, a murky blackness that seemed almost alive, dense and waiting.

Then he felt it – a rush of cold air, sharper than any winter wind, brushing past him like a hand sliding over his skin, raising the fine hairs on his neck. He staggered back, spinning around, but there was nothing behind him. Only the room, silent and still.

The voice in his head was silent now too, the strange chants cut off abruptly, leaving an echoing void in his mind. He turned back to the door, feeling something in him go still, almost numb. His gaze locked onto the hallway that stretched beyond, its walls narrow and looming, painted in some awful shade of greyish brown that might have once been cream or white. Faint stains ran down the walls, dark rivulets that hinted at water damage – or something darker. He shuddered, caught between curiosity and an instinctive urge to flee.

But the darkness called to him, like a hand reaching out, inviting. He leaned closer, squinting into the murk. Strange visions crept into his mind unbidden – images of a room at the end of the hallway, papered in the same dismal brown, its corners damp and crawling with rot. And in the dim light of his imagination, he could almost see stains tracing lines down the walls, dripping to the floor in dark patches that could have been brain matter, blood, something no human should ever see.

The thrill returned, fierce and sharp, buzzing through him with an intensity that nearly sent him to his knees. His breath came quick, each exhale mingling with the stale air wafting out of the tiny opening. He didn't know exactly what lay beyond.

FALLEN RIDGE

But that only made it worse – or maybe better, in a sickening sort of way. He had to know.

Sawyer... my Sawyer, come into my drum... together we'll drink blood like rum...

Ignoring the way his hands shook, Sawyer pushed himself through the door. The space was impossibly narrow; the walls pressing in on either side, and for a terrible moment, he thought he was stuck, wedged halfway in and halfway out, a grotesque decoration dangling from the little door.

With a heave and a grunt, he forced himself forward, feeling the rough edges of the frame scrape against his back and shoulders. Finally, he was through, crouched in the narrow passage, the dark pressing close, almost suffocating. He let out a shaky breath, his heart pounding in his ears, each beat echoing in the silence.

He leaned forward, edging deeper into the darkness, his fingers brushing the walls. They were damp; something sticky clung to his skin – a thin, viscous coating that sent a chill through his bones. He could barely breathe, the air thick and stale, each inhale tinged with that awful smell of decay.

Paul was halfway down the passage when he felt it – a tug on his coat collar, icy fingers brushing the nape of his neck. He froze, every nerve alive with a terror so fierce it felt like fire racing through his veins.

Slowly, he turned, straining to see in the darkness. And there, just inches from his face, two eyes glowed – a sickly, dark red, gleaming with malice, set above a mouth full of teeth that were too sharp, too white, grinning with a hunger that went beyond humour.

Fresh meat, it hissed, the words slithering into Sawyer's mind that scraped like bone against bone.

Sawyer's throat tightened, his body frozen, his mind reeling with a horror that went beyond any simple fear. This was a primal terror, something deep and ancient, a darkness that had waited, biding its time, for someone foolish enough to open the door.

"*Damn*," he whispered, his voice barely audible.

The thing in the darkness lunged, its grip tightening, its fingers pressing into his skin. He screamed, the sound swallowed by the shadows as it dragged him deeper, his body thrashing, his mind clawing for escape, for some impossible salvation.

But the door was already swinging shut, creaking with a finality that echoed in the silent room. And as it clicked into place, the house fell quiet, the only sound the faint, fading echo of Sawyer's scream as he was pulled into the darkness, disappearing into the void, leaving nothing behind but the chill in the air and the awful, unyielding silence.

"I'm not too sure I like this place, Sam," Wendy said, her voice barely louder than a whisper as she rubbed her thin arms, trying to ward off the chill that seemed to seep from the very walls. Her eyes darted around, taking in the shadows that gathered in every corner, each one stretching and writhing as though stirred by a hidden life.

"It's just a little cold, that's all," Sam replied, his voice dripping with a serene confidence that grated against Wendy's unease. He chuckled softly, glancing up at the high, vaulted ceiling where cobwebs hung in thick, draping strands, shimmering like a predator's web, spun to ensnare. "It's dark and dramatic. Very... atmospheric."

"It's... *something*," she murmured, her gaze lingering on a stain that had seeped into the wooden floorboards, dark and ancient, as if something had once bled into the very grain of the wood. A chill ran through her, and she couldn't shake the feeling that she was being watched, that something hungry and patient waited just out of sight.

Mabel Hunter, standing a few steps behind them, offered a tight smile. She'd heard this conversation countless times over the years – new clients, full of curiosity or bravado, who would slowly crumble under the house's relentless sense of decay, a chill that settled into their bones, lingering like a buried memory. Mabel knew exactly what Wendy was feeling: the discomfort creeping up her spine, the prickling unease that made the hair on her arms stand on end. She'd seen it before in every set of eyes that dared to enter the house.

Wendy was looking at her now, her expression a mixture of hope and fear, as though Mabel might offer some reassurance, something to calm the quiet terror blooming in her heart.

Mabel's smile grew a little sadder, almost apologetic. "This house... it's full of history," she said simply, her gaze shifting to the small, sealed door nestled in the centre of the east wall. It looked innocuous enough, yet it seemed to hold an unnatural gravity, pulling her attention back to it repeatedly.

A vague sense of dread settled in her chest as she stared at it, her mind flickering back to an unsettling memory—a man's voice, polite but firm: *Not mojo, Mrs. Hunter. Paranormal activity*.

The words echoed in her head, bringing with them the faintest hint of a memory – green eyes, a leather-bound notebook, the quiet confidence of a man who thought he'd seen it all. His name danced on the edge of her mind, just out of reach, as if it had been erased, leaving only a ghostly afterimage, a trace of something that no longer existed.

She glanced back at her clients, who had wandered towards the windows, talking in hushed tones as they gazed out into the bleak, overgrown gardens. The townsite of Fallen Ridge loomed just below them in the valley. Mabel took a step closer to the door, positioning herself between it and her clients, shielding it almost instinctively, as though some part of her knew that whatever lay beyond should never be disturbed.

But she couldn't stop herself from looking at it. Gooseflesh rose on her arms as she heard the faint, almost inaudible scratching sound drifting from the other side. She wondered, briefly, if she was going mad, if the house had finally sunk its claws into her mind after all these years.

Then the whispers started.

Help me, Mrs. Hunter... are you there?

The voice was faint, as though calling from a place far beyond her reach, but she recognised it. A shiver raced down her spine, settling cold and heavy in her stomach.

"*Paul...*" she whispered, and the name slipped from her lips unbidden, dredged up from some dark corner of her mind. She clutched her coat tighter around herself, her fingers trembling as she took a slow step back from the door.

Help me, Mrs. Hunter... I'm so scared... it's so dark here...

The voice was low, a rasping murmur that slithered into her ears, threading itself into her thoughts with a sickly sweetness. Her mouth went dry, and she felt the prickling sting of tears in her eyes, a deep, visceral sorrow clawing at her chest.

"Oh, *Paul*," she whispered, barely aware of the tears tracing lines down her face, her lips trembling as she stared at the door.

From the other side, the creature that had once been Paul Sawyer continued to whisper, its voice raw and broken, a hollow echo of the man who had once been so certain, so alive.

Please, Mrs. Hunter... let me out. I'm so lonely. Won't you come play with me? Won't you come dream with me?

Its long, gnarled fingernails scraped against the wood, a slow, rhythmic sound that seemed to pulse in time with Mabel's heartbeat. She could almost see him now, in her mind's eye – his twisted form crouched just beyond the door, his hair matted and streaked, hanging over a face that had been warped by endless torment. His skin – if it could still be called that – was peeled and torn, his flesh rotting from the inside out, seething with insects, maggots, and worms that burrowed through his body in endless, writhing loops.

It's not hell, Mrs. Hunter... and it's not death. It's time. Endless time... it devours you from the core outward. It feeds on you, grows in you, until there's nothing left. Come play with time, Mrs. Hunter. Come...

Her breath hitched, a strangled sob escaping her lips as she stumbled back from the door. She clutched a hand to her chest, feeling her heart hammering beneath her ribs, each beat painful, as though it were trying to claw its way out.

But the voice kept coming, relentless, hungry.

Time is coming again, Mrs. Hunter. And it'll feed... oh, it'll feed on me...

The words twisted, warping into a guttural moan of agony, and Mabel could almost see it – the twisted, ravaged form of what had once been Paul Sawyer, his flesh tearing away under the relentless, gnashing teeth of something unseen, something that moved in the darkness like a shadow, something ancient and patient that fed on every second of his suffering, every shuddering breath, every flicker of hope snuffed out under the weight of eternity.

He clawed at his own face, his fingernails raking through the rotting flesh as he wailed, his cries muffled, unheard beyond the narrow door that held him prisoner. Behind him, the darkness shifted, an ever-present figure lurking just beyond his sight, its form a mass of shadows and whispers, a figure that had no shape, no name, only hunger.

In that moment, Mabel felt it – an oppressive weight, a presence that seemed to reach out from beyond the door, pressing down on her, filling her lungs with a thick, suffocating dread. She staggered, gasping for breath, her vision swimming as she fought the urge to scream, to tear herself away from the house and run until she could no longer feel its chilling grasp.

But she couldn't move. She stood rooted to the spot, her eyes fixed on the door, her mind echoing with the whispers that seeped through, desperate and pleading, yet tinged with a darkness that made her skin crawl.

Let me out, Mrs. Hunter... it's so lonely... I'm so scared...

The voice was fading now, sinking into a low, keening wail that seemed to stretch on and on, until it became nothing more than a distant hum, a faint echo lost in the depths of the house.

And then, silence.

Mabel took a shuddering breath, her eyes glassy as she looked around the room, trying to shake the lingering sense of dread that clung to her like mist on a wintry morning. She blinked, feeling as though she'd awoken from a nightmare, a strange, cold clarity settling over her as she forced herself to breathe, to focus.

Mabel looked back at the door, now quiet, the scratches and whispers nothing more than a memory, fading like a half-forgotten dream. She straightened her shoulders, brushing a tear from her cheek, and turned to her clients, who were still gazing out the window, oblivious to the horrors lurking just beyond the thin walls.

"Well," she said, her voice steady, as though nothing at all had happened. "Shall we move on?"

Behind her, from the other side of the sealed door, a single, faint whisper drifted out, soft and desperate, lost in the silence that had settled over the room.

Please... Mrs. Hunter... let me out.

But the house swallowed the sound, burying it in layers of time, sealing it away like a forgotten secret, hidden in the dark where no one would ever find it again.

As Mabel led her clients out, closing the door behind them, the whisper faded into silence, trapped in the endless passage of time, waiting, as the shadows gathered, patient and hungry.

Chapter Four

MAMA

For years after her child's death, Daisy stayed in her mother's house, where every inch seemed saturated with memories. Often, she'd sit on the bathtub's edge, staring at the porcelain sink, recalling the night her baby's wails pierced the silence, louder than the rush of water. She never let herself finish the memory. Though her mother rarely spoke of that night, Daisy could feel the old woman's eyes trailing her, sharp with suspicion and silent contempt – cutting deeper than words.

After her mother died, Daisy didn't sell the house. She couldn't bring herself to leave; the place reeked of the past, yet it was all she had. Fallen Ridge was an insular town, a closed-off world where no one easily escaped their history. Daisy was bound to the town like the roots of the oldest trees, and the house held her still tighter.

When her mother passed, Daisy became its sole inhabitant. She spent most of her time in silence, save for the creak of floorboards and the whispers of wind slipping through the drafty windows. The entire house seemed to hold its breath, as though waiting. And Daisy felt it too – a constant, unyielding dread weighed on her, pressing heavily into her lungs with each breath.

Then, the strange occurrences intensified.

At first, they were small, almost imperceptible – a faint sound of crying that came late at night, so soft she wondered if it was the wind or an echo of her memory. She tried to brush it off, telling herself it was only her mind playing tricks, tangled in guilt. But then came the smell – an acrid, sickly odour that reminded her of sour milk and rotting fruit, creeping through the rooms like a stain. No matter how often she scrubbed, the smell lingered, sour and relentless.

One evening, as she lay in bed, the crying began again, faint and wavering, but unmistakable. She sat up, her heart pounding in her chest, and strained to listen, holding her breath as the sound drifted through the house. A child's cry, soft and pleading, each note laced with despair.

It couldn't be real. She was alone. She knew she was alone. And yet, the sound persisted, growing louder, echoing through the silence until it filled every corner of the house.

Unable to bear it, she flung open her bedroom door and hurried down the hallway, her footsteps loud in the silence. She followed the sound, her pulse racing as she moved closer to the source, her mind filled with a growing sense of dread. The crying led her to the kitchen, and there, on the counter, she found something that made her blood run cold.

A small, damp handprint pressed into the surface of the countertop.

She stared at it, her breath hitching as she took a step back, her heart pounding in her chest. It was *impossible*. She was alone in the house. Yet, the handprint remained, stark and unmistakable – a mark of something beyond her understanding.

She reached out, her fingers trembling as she traced the outline of the handprint, feeling the cold, damp surface beneath her touch. It was real. Tangible. Terror filled her, so profound it felt as if the floor were slipping away, as if she were sinking into darkness.

And then, as suddenly as it had begun, the crying stopped, leaving her alone in the silence, her heart racing as she stared at the empty countertop.

For a long time, she stood there, her mind racing as she tried to make sense of what she had just experienced. But no explanation came. Only silence, thick and oppressive, pressing down on her like a weight.

She fled the kitchen, her footsteps echoing through the empty house as she rushed to her room, her mind spiralling with fear and confusion. She locked the door behind her, her hands shaking as she pressed her back against the door, her heart racing in her chest.

The house was silent, but Daisy felt a presence, a darkness that seemed to seep from the walls themselves, filling the room with a suffocating weight. She could feel it watching her, waiting, and she knew, with a certainty that chilled her to the bone, that she was not alone.

The next morning, Daisy awoke to find the handprint gone. She searched the kitchen, her fingers tracing the surface of the countertop, but there was no sign of the mark. She might almost have believed it had been a dream, an illusion, if not for the faint, lingering odour of sour milk and rot – a smell unmistakable in its persistence.

Daisy tried to lose herself in the mundane routine of her job at the grocer's, immersing herself in the comforting predictability of stocking shelves and manning the till. But even there, shadows from her past seemed to follow her, stretching their reach into the bright, familiar aisles. The rows of shelves seemed longer than usual, the harsh overhead lights flickering intermittently, casting unsettling shadows as she rang up items for silent, staring customers. Each glance at the clock sent a chill down her spine as the minutes dragged by, stretching into an eternity.

Then, as she stood at the register, something caught her eye. At the far end of an aisle stood a small child, his head bowed so that his face hid in the shadows. His clothes were soddened, clinging to his slight frame, his tiny hands hanging limply by his sides. A wave of icy dread surged through her as she instinctively stepped back, her heartbeat loud in her ears.

The child slowly lifted his head, his eyes hollow and expressionless, fixed intently on her. Daisy's breath caught in her throat as their gazes met, and in that vacant stare, she felt an overwhelming weight – a sorrow too old for his slight form, a simmering anger, and a silent accusation. She wanted to look away, to tear herself free from his gaze, but her limbs refused to move, her body paralysed as darkness seemed to close in around her, dragging her downwards as though into some bottomless pit.

Then, in an instant, he was gone. The aisle was empty again, leaving her alone in the silence, her heart pounding as she stared at the vacant space where he had been.

That day, she fled the store, her mind awash with fear and confusion. The visions, the smells, the handprint – they were real. And they were consuming her, pulling her deeper into the dark waters of her own guilt and regret, with a force that felt impossible to escape.

The haunting grew worse in the days that followed. Each night, Daisy lay in bed, listening to faint cries drifting through the house – small, desperate sounds that made her skin crawl and filled her with a dread so heavy it seemed to press her into the mattress. She kept the windows open, hoping the chill night air would clear the house of the lingering smell, the shadows, the memories. But nothing seemed to help.

One night, as she lay in the darkness, the cries grew louder, turning sharp and insistent, echoing through the silence until they seeped into every corner of the room. She covered her ears and squeezed her eyes shut, trying to push the sounds away, but they pressed in on her, slipping through her defences. Her chest tightened with terror, a cold and consuming dread.

Then, she felt it – a weight pressing down on her chest, cold and unrelenting, stealing her breath. Her heart hammered as she opened her eyes, and there, hovering above her, she saw him.

Her son.

His small face hovered before her, pale and twisted in sorrow. His eyes, dark and unfathomable, seemed to pierce her as though seeing everything inside her – all her fears, her regrets, her secrets. He reached out, his tiny fingers brushing her skin, and she felt a chill so sharp it seemed to slice through her, freezing her to the core.

Daisy wanted to scream, to pull away, but her body refused to obey. She was trapped by his gaze, his touch, his presence, bound to him by something deeper than fear.

In the silence, his voice broke through – a whisper, soft yet piercing, filling her mind and her heart with a single, accusing question.

"Why, Mama? Why did you do it?"

The words hung between them, heavy and unanswerable, and she lay there paralysed, her heart pounding, her mind spiralling through fear and regret. She wanted to answer, to find some way to explain, but her throat closed under the weight of her guilt, strangling the words before they could form.

And as the darkness closed in around her, Daisy understood the awful truth – she would never be free. She was a prisoner, condemned to live in the shadows of her past, bound forever by the sins she couldn't outrun.

Daisy could barely bring herself to return to the grocery store the next morning. Each step felt heavier, as though shadows clung to her heels, dragging her back. Ridley's Market looked the same as ever: shelves lined with tins of soup, bottles of fizzy drink, sacks of flour – all ordinary things that now seemed bleak under the harsh fluorescent lights. She avoided the customers' eyes, keeping her head down as she stacked shelves, the clatter of tins masking the relentless thud of her heartbeat.

The store was nearly empty, apart from the usual regulars – Mrs. Halloway, who spent more time in the produce section than buying anything, and old Mr. Jenson, who lingered near the freezers, muttering under his breath. They were harmless, familiar faces, yet Daisy felt an urgent need to escape, as though her very skin was itching to leave. She kept glancing over her shoulder, half-expecting to see her son's ghostly figure trailing behind her, the haunting image that had intruded even into her waking hours.

But he wasn't there. Only the aisles stretched before her, filled with food and cleaning supplies, tools and toys – a catalogue of the ordinary things people needed to survive. And yet, these objects seemed to observe her, each one bearing silent witness to her secret, to the darkness she carried.

Then, as she moved down the row of canned goods, a scent filled the air – a smell familiar and chilling. The faint stench of sour milk lingered around her, clinging thickly to the air like fog. She froze, her pulse quickening as the smell intensified, filling her nose and making her stomach churn.

A soft cry drifted through the stillness, faint and tremulous, yet unmistakable. Daisy's heart jolted as she turned, scanning the empty aisle behind her. The crying grew louder, each sound laced with despair, and she took a step back, her fingers gripping the edge of the shelf to steady herself.

"Daisy?" a voice asked softly from behind her.

She spun around, her pulse racing, to see Mrs. Halloway standing there, her face lined with concern. "Are you all right, dear?" Mrs. Halloway asked, her voice gentle, her gaze soft.

Daisy tried to reply, to force a polite smile or a nod, but her voice caught in her throat, tangled with the fear that constricted her chest, cold and unrelenting.

"Daisy?" Mrs. Halloway's brow creased, and she took a step closer, extending a hand as though to offer comfort.

The cry came again, louder this time – a thin, desperate wail that seemed to seep into the air itself. Daisy flinched, her heart pounding as she looked back over her shoulder at the empty aisle. She could feel him there.

"Daisy, you look like you've seen a *ghost*," Mrs. Halloway murmured, her voice soft, almost pitying.

For a fleeting moment, anger flared inside her, hot and bitter, bubbling up from the depths of her fear. Seen a ghost? She wanted to scream, to tear at her own skin, to let the world see the horror that clung to her, dogging her steps. But as quickly as the anger surfaced, it dissolved, leaving her hollow, weighed down by a crushing sense of despair.

"I... I need some air," Daisy managed, her voice shaking, and before Mrs. Halloway could respond, she turned and fled, her footsteps echoing down the empty aisles as she hurried towards the exit.

Outside, the air hung thick and humid, the sky overcast, the town shrouded in a grey haze that settled over the buildings like a damp shroud. Daisy leaned against the wall, her heart racing as she fought to steady her breath, her mind tangled with fear and confusion.

She couldn't go on like this. She couldn't keep running, hiding, burying herself in shadows. The cries, the handprints, the whispers – they were all real, fragments of the darkness she carried. And she knew, now, that the past never truly dies.

That night, as Daisy lay in bed, the cries began again – soft, plaintive sounds that drifted through the darkness, filling the room with a chill that seeped into her bones. She gripped the edges of the quilt, her knuckles white, her heart hammering as the sound grew louder, more insistent, reverberating through the silence until it seemed to inhabit every shadowed corner.

"*Please...* please *stop...*" she whispered, her voice shaking as she pressed her hands over her ears, desperate to shut out the sound.

But the cries only grew, piercing through her defences, dismantling the walls she had tried so hard to build around her heart. Each note seemed filled with sorrow, tinged with an accusation that made her chest tighten.

Then, in the thick darkness, she heard his voice – a soft, pleading murmur that drifted through the silence.

"Why, Mama? Why did you do it?"

The question lingered, heavy and unyielding, pressing down on her.

"I... I didn't mean to..." she managed, her voice barely more than a whisper, the words catching in her throat as her guilt and fear coiled tightly around her, pressing on her chest.

But the voice was relentless, each word a deeper, colder blade slicing through her already fragile heart.

"Why, Mama? Why did you kill me?"

She couldn't answer. She couldn't bear to speak, to confront the horror, the inescapable truth of what she had done. As the cries grew louder, more anguished, she felt herself sinking, drowning in a suffocating tide of guilt and regret – a darkness so deep it threatened to swallow her whole.

Days blurred into nights, and nights turned into waking nightmares for Daisy. She moved through life in a fog, trapped in a relentless purgatory that clung to her like a second skin. The boundary between reality and the haunting dissolved, leaving her trapped in an endless loop of work, dread, and the terrible sounds that greeted her each time she returned to her empty house. The cries and whispers now followed her everywhere – haunting the aisles of the grocery store, echoing from the drains on every street, even surfacing in her thoughts when she tried to sleep.

She grew hollow. Her skin turned pale and drawn, her eyes circled by dark shadows, her movements slowed to a mechanical drift. The townsfolk noticed. They watched her, some with pity, others with suspicion. The whispers about her past grew louder, filling the empty spaces she left behind. She didn't need to hear the words to know what they said: that she was cursed, haunted, that her sins had finally come to collect.

And Daisy knew they were right.

One night, after another long day at the store, Daisy returned to her house, her steps heavy, her heart pounding with the familiar dread that greeted her at the door. The stench hit her first – a sharp, sour odour that clung to the walls, coating the air in a thick, nauseating heaviness. She gagged, pressing a hand over her mouth as she stumbled down the darkened hallway, her mind muddled with fear and exhaustion.

She didn't bother with the lights. It didn't matter; darkness or light, the thing that haunted her remained unchanged, its presence woven into every shadow, every silent corner.

In the stillness, she heard it – a faint, rhythmic sound, like soft, bare footsteps on the floorboards. Her heart stilled, then thundered, her blood running cold as she froze in place, her breath caught in her throat. The sound grew louder, each step deliberate, steady, carrying a weight that made her shiver.

She knew what she would see, but the knowing did nothing to ease the horror. Slowly, she turned, her gaze drawn to the darkness at the end of the hallway.

There, shrouded in shadows, stood her son. His slight form seemed almost to blend with the darkness, his face obscured, his head tilted as if watching her.

Daisy's pulse quickened, her body rigid with fear. She wanted to scream, to flee, but she was rooted in place, trapped under the weight of his gaze, unable to look away from the figure before her.

"*Why*, Mama?" he asked, his voice soft, a fragile murmur that cut through the silence. Each word held a sorrow so deep it seemed to press against her chest, constricting her breath. "*Why* did you do it?"

The question hung between them, heavy, unyielding, like a stone lodged in her chest.

"I... I didn't mean to..." she managed, her voice barely a whisper, the words catching as her guilt and fear tangled together, pressing down on her like an invisible hand.

But his voice continued, relentless, a thread of sadness woven with accusation that sliced deeper with each word.

"Why, Mama? Why did you *kill* me?"

She couldn't answer. The words died in her throat, too laden with terror, with the weight of what she had done. As the cries grew louder, more insistent, she felt herself sinking, drowning in the dark tide of her own guilt and regret – a darkness so profound it threatened to pull her under completely.

The figure took a step closer, his small, bare feet soundless against the floor, his face veiled in shadow, his gaze locked on her with a cold, unyielding intensity.

"Why, Mama?" he asked again, his voice softer, each word resonating in the silence like a wound reopening. The sorrow in his voice seemed to pass through her, piercing into places she couldn't reach, tearing at her from within.

"I didn't mean to..." she choked out, her voice a frail whisper.

But he only stared at her, his gaze empty, a hollow darkness that seemed to stretch endlessly, drawing her into its depths.

She took a shaky step back, her heart pounding as she stumbled through the hallway, her mind spiralling in a frenzy of fear and despair. She fled into her bedroom, slamming the door behind her, her hands shaking as she locked it, her breath coming in short, ragged gasps.

But she knew the lock wouldn't keep him out. Nothing would.

Silence filled the room, thick and oppressive. She clutched the edge of the bed; her knuckles white, her heart pounding as she waited, every fibre of her tense with anticipation.

Then, breaking the stillness, came the faint, rhythmic sound of his footsteps, growing closer, until they stopped just outside her door.

She held her breath, her body trembling, her heart a frantic drumbeat in her chest.

The doorknob rattled, the sound sharp, piercing the quiet, and Daisy clamped her hands over her ears, squeezing her eyes shut, willing herself not to hear, not to believe.

But the door creaked open, spilling cold air into the room, a chill that seeped into her bones, sharp and unforgiving.

In the doorway stood her son, silhouetted in the dim light, his gaze locked onto hers with that same unyielding intensity.

"Why, Mama?" he asked, his voice soft, each word imbued with a sorrow that tore through her, hollowing her out.

Daisy's breath caught, her body rigid with fear, her heart pounding in her chest.

"I'm sorry..." she whispered, her voice barely audible, the words slipping out like a confession, a desperate plea for forgiveness that she knew would never come.

But the figure only stared, his gaze as empty as it was dark, drawing her into an abyss that she feared she would never escape.

Daisy stopped going to work. She couldn't bear the whispers of the townsfolk, their sharp glances, their pity. Ridley's Market, once just a part of her routine, had turned into a place of nightmares, every aisle a corridor of painful reminders. She barely slept, barely ate. Her world had shrunk down to the four walls of her old house, a tomb of her own making. Days blurred as she drifted through hours of silence, haunted by faint, mournful cries that seeped through the house, each one a reminder of the tiny life she had taken.

The air inside grew thick, stifling, like the stagnant breath of something long buried. The stench of sour milk and rot was stronger than ever, clinging to every surface, settling into her skin with each laboured breath. It was as if the house itself had decayed, mirroring the darkness that had taken root in her soul.

Each night, he was there. Waiting for her in the shadows, his small, pale face staring up at her, eyes hollow yet filled with a sorrow that seemed to pierce her very core. He would stand silently at the edge of her bed, watching, his gaze heavy with accusation.

One night, unable to bear the silence any longer, she spoke.

"*Please*," she whispered, her voice barely more than a tremor. Her heart thudded painfully; her hands clenched into fists beneath the quilt. "*Please*... let me go. I'm sorry... I didn't mean to... I was just so... so *tired*..."

But he only stared, his unblinking gaze fixed on her, his small hands limp at his sides.

"Why, Mama?" he asked, his voice soft, pleading, each word carrying a weight that settled deep in her chest. "Why did you kill me?"

"I'm sorry..." she choked out, her voice thin, almost lost.

But the figure did not move. His gaze remained cold, empty, cutting through her like a winter wind.

Slowly, he reached out, his small hand brushing against her cheek. His touch was ice, sending a shock through her body that made her shiver, every nerve alight with dread.

Daisy screamed, the sound tearing from her throat, raw and desperate. She knew she couldn't take it anymore.

The next day, Daisy went to the edge of town, to the church. She hadn't set foot there since her son's funeral; the place held too many reminders of her sins. But now she was desperate. She couldn't continue like this, couldn't bear the weight of her guilt pressing down on her day after day. She needed help – needed someone to listen, to understand.

Daisy stepped inside, her footsteps echoing faintly in the stillness. Her gaze settled on the altar at the far end of the room. She felt the eyes of the saints staring down at her from their statues, their faces cold, filled with silent judgment. She kept her focus straight ahead, moving toward the confessional, her heart hammering as she slid into the narrow, darkened space.

For a long moment, she sat in silence, her hands clasped tightly in her lap, her breath unsteady, caught between fear and desperation. Then, in a voice barely above a whisper, she spoke.

"Forgive me, Father, for I have sinned," she murmured, her voice trembling, the words slipping out like a plea, a fragile attempt to release the horror that had taken hold of her.

Pastor Lou's voice drifted through the screen, low and weary. "Tell me, my child. What burdens your soul?"

She swallowed, her throat tightening, memories of that night clawing their way to the surface. She could almost feel the darkness within her, like a shadow taking root, entwining itself with every breath.

"I... I killed my son," she whispered, the words barely audible, leaking out as though they might poison the air. "I was... I was young, alone... I didn't know what to do. He wouldn't stop crying... he wouldn't let me sleep... I just wanted it to stop."

Her voice broke, a sob slipping through as if it had been trapped inside her for years.

Pastor Lou remained silent; his presence quiet but unyielding. She could see him now, his head bowed, his hands folded. A deep sorrow flickered in his gaze, and for a moment, she thought she saw the glimmer of understanding there, a shadow of his own burdens.

"You've carried this alone for a long time, haven't you?" he asked finally, his voice gentle, void of judgment.

She nodded, her breath hitching, the weight of her confession settling over her like a leaden cloak.

"But I don't... I don't know how to let go," she whispered, her voice trembling. "He haunts me... every night... he's there, waiting, watching."

The priest was silent for a long moment, his expression unreadable as he looked upwards, as though seeking guidance in the dim light.

"Sometimes, the dead linger," he said at last, his voice quiet. "They carry with them the weight of unfinished business, of sorrows that bind them to this world. And sometimes... sometimes... they seek justice."

Daisy's heart skipped, a chill rippling through her as the meaning of his words sank in.

"But what... what can I do?" she asked, her voice a faint thread, a desperate plea that barely held together. "How do I make him leave?"

Pastor Lou's gaze softened, and he looked at her with a glistening in his eyes, a hint of grief that he held close, unspoken.

"Sometimes, there's no way to make them leave," he said, his voice wavering. "Sometimes, the only way to find peace... is to face them, to confront the darkness that lives inside you."

That night, Daisy returned to her house, her heart racing, her mind awash in equal parts fear and determination. She was tired of running, tired of hiding, tired of burying herself in shadows.

She was ready to face him – to confront the darkness that had taken root within her.

As she stepped inside, the stench of sour milk and rot flooded her senses, stronger than ever, clinging to her like damp fabric. She didn't turn on the lights, didn't seek the comfort of familiar things. She needed to face the truth, to confront the horror she had avoided for so long.

Her footsteps echoed as she moved towards the kitchen, her gaze locking onto the sink, where her life had irreversibly changed. Each step felt like descending deeper into an abyss, memories resurfacing with brutal clarity, sharper and more vivid than ever.

The darkness thickened around her, filling the room with a chill that seeped into her bones, so cold it felt as though she were standing in her own grave. And then she saw him – standing in the doorway, his small, pale face lifted towards her, his eyes hollow, seeming to pierce straight through her.

"Why, Mama?" he asked, his voice barely more than a murmur. "Why did you kill me?"

Daisy's breath faltered. She took a step back, her body trembling, her throat constricting around the words that tried to escape.

"I didn't mean to..." she whispered, her voice frail and cracked, each word barely more than a breath.

Her son took a slow step closer, his bare feet soundless on the floor, his face slipping into shadow, his gaze fixed on her with an intensity that felt as if it could strip her soul bare.

For a moment, her eyes caught her own reflection in the window – a face twisted with horror, her eyes wide, glassy with fear. Her gaze held there, drawn to her son's reflection beside her. In the glass, his face was drained of life, his skin ashen, his eyes dark and empty, brimming with silent accusation. He looked right at her, his mouth moving soundlessly before his voice filled her mind.

"Why did you kill me, Mama?" he repeated, his voice a soft whisper that pierced through her like needles of ice.

Daisy stumbled back, clutching the edge of the counter as though it might hold her upright, her fingers slipping against the cold, damp surface. She wanted to turn away, to break free from the sight in the window, but something rooted her to the spot – a presence darker, unknowable, lurking in the shadows behind her son.

A shape emerged, an ink-blackness bleeding into the reflection like a stain spreading across glass. Her pulse pounded in her throat as realisation dawned: something else was there, lurking just behind her son's ghostly form. A face appeared, pale and grinning, its mouth stretched unnaturally wide in a smile that seemed carved into the skin, revealing rows of yellowed, rotting teeth that spiralled into an endless dark void. Its eyes, two pits of gleaming red, fixed on her with a hunger that turned her insides to ice.

The demon's grin widened as though savouring her terror. Slowly, it lifted a skeletal finger, pointing directly at her, an invitation she didn't want to accept.

Daisy gasped, cold air freezing in her lungs, her mouth opening in a silent scream. The room pressed in around her, thickening as though invisible hands were tightening around her, and a foul, decayed stench filled her nostrils – a smell that seemed to come from something long dead and restless. In the glass, her son laughed, a dry, hollow sound, cracking through the silence like branches snapping underfoot.

And then – *oh God, no* – she saw her own face in the glass, her mouth stretched into a scream, her eyes wide with a terror that hollowed them. The demon's long, bony fingers rose higher, reaching towards her reflection, twisting and elongating as they wrapped around her reflected throat, pressing closer and closer until she felt the cold weight around her own neck, squeezing the breath from her body.

With a final, shuddering inhale, Daisy felt the demon's eyes bore into her, as though it were unravelling every hidden part of her. Its mouth widened, an endless, gaping chasm, and Daisy felt her own mouth mirror it, forced open, her jaw stretching impossibly wide, beyond what should have been possible.

Then she felt it – a pressure, cold and slimy, pressing against her lips, forcing its way down her throat. Daisy gagged, clawing at her own neck, but her body betrayed her, refusing to obey. She couldn't stop it; she couldn't even move. The demon was crawling into her, inch by inch, filling her, its laughter echoing in her mind as it claimed her flesh, her spirit, her very self.

Through the haze of terror, she glimpsed her reflection in the glass one last time. Her face had twisted into something monstrous, her eyes blackened and hollow, her mouth curled into a hideous grin that wasn't her own. And beside her, her son reached up and took her hand, his small fingers curling into hers, pulling her down, down into darkness.

"Now you're mine, Mama."

The last sound she heard was Pastor Lou's voice, soft and distant, "...sometimes... they seek justice."

Chapter Five

THE WIDOW

THE LARKIN HOUSE STOOD at the edge of Fallen Ridge like a relic, a weathered monument steeped in death and madness. Built when the land was still unclaimed, when people believed they owned the earth simply because they walked upon it, the house was a Victorian edifice with Gothic inclinations – its sharp turrets rose like witching spires, its arched windows seemed to scowl, and its black shutters, twisted and peeling, hung like ragged claws. Everything about the house suggested it had witnessed horrors. And it had.

Margaret Larkin was as much a part of the house as its walls, worn and as unyielding as its beams. She had outlasted three husbands, each one claimed by circumstances the town muttered about only in shadows. They called her a witch; they said she was cursed. In some ways, they weren't wrong.

Margaret's curse, however, wasn't just a rumour – it was something she felt in her very bones. Haunted not by the memories of her dead husbands, but by the men themselves, their faces appeared in mirrors, contorted by fury, grief, and regret. Each one remained shackled to her by a force she barely understood, bound to her within the darkness of that rotting house. Wherever she went within those walls, she felt them there, tasted their bitterness in the back of her throat as if it were a draught of poison. She had tried everything she could think of to break their hold – rituals of blood and candlelight, whispered prayers to gods with forgotten names, offerings left at altars worn smooth by despair. Yet nothing had set her free. She was as much their prisoner as they were hers.

More and more, she suspected the curse had nothing to do with the house itself, but lay within her very blood, like a sickness passed through her veins.

Elijah had been her first husband, her first real taste of passion and, soon after, her first taste of cruelty. Young and untamed, he swept her off her feet with a vigour that left her feeling more alive than she'd ever known. They married quickly and lived faster still, moving into the old house, filling it with the sound of arguments, laughter, and broken promises. But the fire that had drawn them together soon burned out, leaving only cold ash that choked rather than warmed, and in that ash, something darker festered – a rage that both thrilled and terrified her.

One night, during a storm that shook the house as if its very foundations were being rattled beneath a torrent, Elijah went out for a walk and never returned. She told the town as much, but few believed her. The people of the Ridge knew Elijah wasn't the type to simply walk away, and Margaret wasn't the type to simply wait. They whispered of dark deeds; of things she might have done to keep him bound to the land. They searched the property, found nothing, but the house was a keeper of secrets, a place where truths could hide in plain sight.

On the lonely nights that followed his disappearance, she saw him in the mirrors. At first, it seemed a trick of the light – a fleeting shadow, a murky form too dark to be her own reflection. But then he was there, unmistakable: his face pale, his skin drawn tight like a mask stretched over something grotesque. His mouth was twisted open, as if frozen in a silent scream, and his

FALLEN RIDGE

eyes – black and fathomless – seethed with a rage that felt like it could burn through the glass itself. Those eyes followed her, unblinking, filled with a hatred that seeped out and poisoned the very air.

Margaret draped every mirror in the house, yet his presence lingered. She could feel him pressing in from the walls, his essence woven into the air, a weight that smothered her thoughts and settled on her like a shroud. One night, she felt fingers clamp around her ankle, cold and unyielding as iron, dragging her towards the edge of the bed. She kicked and thrashed, screaming until her voice was raw, but when she looked, there was no one there – only the chilling imprint of his fingers left on her skin, like a bruise from beyond.

That night, she struggled to keep her eyes open, terrified that the moment she closed them, he would appear beside her, lying in the bed with his mouth agape and his dead, staring eyes fixed on hers, unblinking.

Charles was nothing like Elijah. Where Elijah had been fire and chaos, Charles was ice and calculation, a man who prized control as much as he valued his business dealings. He was powerful, respected in the community, and he wanted Margaret as his possession, a prize to be claimed. She knew the type well, understood his need to make her submit, to break her spirit without so much as raising his voice. And for a time, she played along, letting him believe he'd won her over.

Their marriage was quiet, cold, stifling. Charles was not a man who shouted or argued; instead, he withdrew, leaving her trapped in a silence more suffocating than any scream. He watched her with eyes as lifeless as embers, his smile as thin and sharp as a blade. Sometimes, Margaret wondered if he suspected what had happened to Elijah, if he sensed the darkness that lingered beneath her surface, something dormant yet potent in her very blood.

One morning, she found him lying cold and blue in their bed, his eyes fixed on nothing, his body rigid with the absolute finality of death. The townsfolk spoke of a heart attack, an ailment they all knew too well, but Margaret felt certain that the house had claimed him. It had fed on his anger, his possessiveness, his relentless need for dominance, and it had devoured him in silence. She could feel him now, an icy fury seeping from the walls, a chill that settled in her bones like winter that would never thaw.

Yet Charles differed from Elijah. Where Elijah was a mere shadow, glimpsed in the edges of mirrors, Charles was a force—imposing, unyielding. He was not content with haunting the glass; he wanted to control even in death. She heard his footsteps echo in empty hallways, felt the cold trace of fingers along her neck, heard his voice whispering her name in the dark, soft but insistent, as though he had never truly left.

One night, she woke to find him standing over her, his eyes dark and hollow, his mouth stretched into a rictus of hatred. He was insubstantial, a figure of smoke and shadows, but his gaze burned with an unnatural heat that made her skin prickle. Leaning down until his face hovered mere inches from hers, he spoke in a voice barely more than a breath, each word laced with venom.

"You thought you could be rid of me, Margaret," he whispered, his voice cold as grave dirt. "But I'm in your blood now. I'm in your bones."

Margaret tried to scream, but he clamped a hand over her mouth, cold and unyielding. She felt his fingers press against her lips, an icy weight that sent shivers of terror through her. She blinked, and he was gone, leaving only the sharp stench of damp earth and decay lingering in the room, clinging to her skin like a chilling reminder of his presence.

William had been her last hope – a man who promised salvation, who spoke of love and redemption as if they were gifts he could give as effortlessly as a whisper. A doctor by trade, he was a man of compassion and healing, and for a while, Margaret almost believed he could lift the shadows that clung to her life. He brought warmth into her world, a gentleness that made her think, just briefly, that perhaps her curse could be broken.

But the house claimed him too. He fell ill, a sickness searing through him like fire, leaving him fevered and delirious, his once gentle eyes now glassy and faraway. She nursed him, fighting to keep him alive, yet the sickness consumed him, leaving her alone once more in the house's embrace.

Unlike the others, William's spirit did not rage or haunt with fury. Instead, he lingered – a presence filled with sorrow so profound it seeped into her, drowning her in despair that pressed down like lead upon her veins. She saw him in the mirrors, his face pale and hollow, his eyes fathomless with grief, his mouth drawn into a sorrowful grimace. He was not angry, but his sorrow was an agony that weighed heavier than any fury, a quiet torment that clung to her like a second skin.

One night, she woke to find him standing at the foot of her bed, his gaze hollow and wet, his expression so full of anguish that it felt as though her heart might crack beneath its weight. He didn't speak; he only stared, his eyes unblinking, his grief wrapping around her like a shroud until she could scarcely draw breath.

"William," she whispered, her voice trembling. "Please, let me go."

But he only shook his head, his sorrow binding her, smothering her, wrapping around her like chains forged from darkness. His presence was an anchor, a shackle that dragged her down deeper into the shadows that filled the house, pulling her further into the despair that had consumed him.

Desperate and afraid, Margaret turned to the darkest pages of her ancient books, seeking release through rituals of blood, fire, and sacrifice. She had nothing left to lose, no hope of escape except through the dark magic that had bound her to the house and the dead who haunted her every step.

As she began the ritual, her voice quivered, a tremor betraying her desperation. The air thickened, heavy with the weight of unseen presences. Shadows on the walls twisted, slowly contorting into faces she knew – Elijah, Charles, William – each one staring at her with eyes filled with fury, grief, and bitter regret. They were all there, tethered to her, their spirits woven deeply into the fabric of the house that held them captive.

She could feel them closing in, icy hands reaching, claws extending, their voices a low, malevolent hum that throbbed in her bones. The candle flames shuddered, casting shadows that pulsed like they were alive, breathing and lurking, waiting to pounce.

Then a voice sliced through the darkness, sharp and cold as a shard of ice.

"Margaret..."

It was Elijah. His voice carried a simmering anger, a betrayal so raw it felt as though it could sear through her. "Did you think you could escape us?"

She turned, but the room was filled with pressing shadows, faces stretching from the walls, their eyes blazing with a rage that made her blood run cold.

"Margaret..." Charles's voice hissed, filled with a cruel sneer. "You belong to us."

"Forever," William murmured, his tone soft but weighted with a sorrow that settled on her like chains, binding her in place.

The shadows loomed closer, pressing against her, pulling her down, and she screamed – a sound swallowed by the consuming darkness as their hands wrapped around her, dragging her into the black, into the endless chill. She felt her spirit fraying, unravelling, merging with the house, drawn into the same dark eternity that had claimed the souls of the men she had loved and lost.

When the sun rose, the house stood silent, empty. Yet, if you looked closely at the windows, if you dared to stare long enough, you might see them—four faces twisted in eternal expressions of rage, sorrow, and despair, trapped forever within the shadows of the Ridge.

Chapter Six

SELFIE

THE ITEM HAD no price tag. In fact, there were no tags on anything in the shop, just a faint scent of old timber and the stubborn dampness that clung to antique furniture.

"How much for this?" Karen asked, fingers resting lightly on the item she'd placed on the counter.

The woman behind the counter – *woman* felt barely appropriate; she looked more like a figure preserved by time – lifted her head with a slow, creaking motion. Wisps of silvery hair clung to her scalp, revealing the sheen of skin beneath, thin and brown, hanging loosely as though gravity had worn it down over the decades. Her eyes... they held a hollowness, a vacancy that only came from seeing too much pain stretched across too many years. The clouded gaze was eerie, as if whatever spirit had once been behind those eyes had departed long ago, leaving only a shell.

She rose from her chair, which protested with a deep groan as she pulled herself upright. Each pop of her joints sounded loud in the quiet, stale air, making Karen flinch. Her arms hung loosely at her sides, bony and slack like the limbs of a scarecrow, her body stooped forward under an invisible burden, as if the weight of her years was drawing her inexorably earthward.

Karen's item – a Polaroid 600 – sat on the counter, black and polished, an odd contrast amidst the dust-laden relics surrounding it. It looked almost new, a surprising relic among the shop's relics. It reminded her of the one her parents used to have, the one that lived on a top shelf in her father's study, waiting for summers, road trips, those rare moments that always seemed too precious to capture. She hadn't realised Polaroid cameras were still around, much less in such good condition. Already, she could feel an old longing tugging at her, a nostalgic pull she hadn't expected, the way one might feel drawn to an old blanket after a nightmare. Even if it didn't work, it would still be worth displaying.

For a moment, she was no longer in the shop. She was back on a beach, squinting against the summer light, her mother's arm wrapped around her shoulder as they beamed into the camera, her father grinning behind it. *Say cheese!* he'd call, his voice warm and familiar, the voice of a man who hadn't yet been overtaken by illness or sorrow. The memory lingered, vivid as a photograph, complete with the soft whirr and click of the Polaroid as it spat out the square snapshot. Little Karen would run over, tugging on her father's sleeve. "Did the camera fairy come, Daddy?" She'd always believed photos were a kind of magic, appearing like gifts in that white-bordered square.

A raspy voice pulled her back to the present. The old woman eyed the camera with a distaste Karen found oddly unsettling, as though the object was tainted. Her hand, thin and veined, hovered toward it but stopped just shy of touching. The hand trembled, then withdrew, and Karen noticed the bruised patches mottling her skin.

"So... *old*," the woman murmured, barely louder than a dry whisper, her gaze fixed on something only she could see, something distant, obscured behind her cataract-clouded eyes.

Karen suppressed a nervous laugh, feeling it bubble up beneath her polite smile. *Old? Well, that's one way to put it*, she thought, feeling a pang of guilt at her own amusement. She forced herself to speak cheerfully.

"Well, no older than the early 1980s, I'd guess?"

The woman's eyes sharpened, and Karen instantly regretted her words. There was a depth to the woman's expression – a sorrow that felt ancient, beyond the memory of any shopkeeper.

A chill crept up Karen's spine, lingering as the word ancient echoed uncomfortably in her mind.

The woman leaned closer, her thin lips parting slightly to reveal a scattering of yellow, uneven teeth, as if rooted in place by sheer stubbornness. "No price. Take it," she said, her voice abrupt, almost a command. She turned away quickly, as if the sight of the camera pained her.

Karen blinked, taken aback. "What?" She laughed, a touch too loudly. "Free? Really? This is an *original* Polaroid 600. These are collector's items. I don't even know if you can buy film for them anymore. Still, it's got to be worth *something*."

In her mind, a warning flared. *Just take the camera and leave, you fool!* But curiosity anchored her in place, a persistent tug that overrode the unease pooling in her stomach.

The woman had paused mid-step, her thin shoulders slumped, as though bearing a weight invisible to anyone else. She turned back slowly, her gaze settling on Karen once more. That chilling look resurfaced, carrying a silent message that seemed to whisper. *I've seen things you'd never believe, my dear.*

"Too old to price," the woman whispered, her voice barely rising above a murmur. "It's free. Just take it."

Karen hesitated, her fingers trembling as she pulled a crumpled fifty-pound note from her purse. She needed this exchange to feel... grounded, ordinary. She wanted to shake off the strange fog that hung over her like a cobweb.

"Here, how about fifty?" she offered, trying to sound casual, hoping to break the oppressive air of the room. "I can't just take it for nothing."

The woman glanced from the note to the camera, her mouth curling into a faint, unsettling smile that cracked the dry skin of her lips. "I told you," she rasped, her voice hollow. "I want nothing for it. Just take it away, and all is well."

Karen's pulse quickened as she tucked the note back in her purse. She couldn't explain it, but it felt as though she was crossing a line, as if accepting this camera meant more than she was prepared to understand.

"Thank you," she managed, her voice strangely hollow as she picked up the Polaroid, her fingers tingling against its cool, smooth edges.

As she reached the door, the woman's voice echoed once more, low and dry, stopping her in her tracks.

"Don't thank me too soon, dear."

Karen glanced back, but the woman had disappeared behind the counter, leaving only the top of her thin, grey hair visible.

"And don't take a picture of yourself," came the voice again, drifting from the shadows like dust motes in the air. "Photograph your cat, your dog, your furniture if you like. But never yourself." She paused, and then added, "And beware of the *eye*."

"The *eye*?" Karen asked, nerves prickling. "Do you mean... the lens?"

A heavy silence stretched between them before the woman's whisper cut through, sharp as a blade.

"No," she said. "I mean the *eye*."

Don't look into the eye...

The words lodged in Karen's mind like a sliver she couldn't quite reach, sharp and festering somewhere deep and irrational. She sat perched on her worn leather sofa in the dim light of her second-floor flat, staring at the Polaroid 600 resting innocuously on the coffee table. It looked harmless... ordinary. Or was it?

Since leaving the shop, the old woman's words had been playing on a loop in her mind, first in her own voice: *Don't look into the eye? What does that mean?* But gradually, it was the woman's brittle whisper that haunted her thoughts, seeping through her mind like cold fog. Karen could almost hear the words, rasping as though the old woman were beside her, breathing them over her shoulder.

"Get a grip, Kaz," she muttered, pressing her fingers to her temples to still the growing ache. *It's just a damn camera.* She chuckled, but the sound felt hollow, floating into the darkened room and dying there. *What harm has a camera ever done to anyone?*

A thought crept up unbidden: *a camera killed Princess Diana...*

FALLEN RIDGE

She winced, a bitter smile forming as she forced herself to dismiss it. No. It was the idiots with cameras who killed her. Shaking her head, she tried to shake off the dark thoughts that clung to her ever since leaving the shop. The thing probably doesn't even work, she told herself. It probably doesn't even have film.

On impulse, she snatched the camera from the table and turned it over in her hands, testing its weight. It felt heavier than she remembered, the plastic and metal oddly cold against her skin, as though it held some ancient chill absorbed. A faint shiver prickled along her arms, but she brushed it off with a smirk. *Idiot*, she thought. *It's just a camera*.

With a decisive click, she popped open the top of the Polaroid; her gaze catching on the glint of the lens – or was it an eye? The way it caught the light made it seem as if it were staring back at her, an unsettling gleam in the dimness, as though aware. She hesitated. Her father's words about old cameras drifted through her mind: Polaroid film is sensitive to light, he'd once told her, his voice warm and distant, a memory preserved from a time before everything went dark.

Almost to prove the thing didn't work, she raised it, pointing it at the far side of the living room. Her finger rested on the shutter release, half in irritation, half in challenge. She pressed the button.

A blinding flash lit up the room, followed by a familiar series of whirrs and clicks that filled the silence. Karen's eyes widened in surprise as the Polaroid spat out a small square of film. It works?

She placed the developing photo on the table, upside down, feeling a thrill of excitement mingle with the lingering unease. The photo lay there, silent and blank, slowly forming in the shadows. She forced herself to wait, counting the seconds. Finally, she flipped it over and stared.

It was perfect – almost *too* perfect – a sharp, clear image of the far side of her living room. Every detail was precise, the picture crisp and flawless, as though taken by a high-definition digital camera rather than an ageing Polaroid. *That's... impossible*, she thought, running her fingers over the image, half expecting the detail to blur under her touch.

"That's... *impressive*," she whispered. She picked up the camera again, inspecting it, her fingers tracing its edges. Her gaze lingered on the lens – the eye, her mind whispered, and an icy prickling crept up her spine.

Don't look into the eye...

Her laugh came too loud, breaking the heavy silence. *Crazy old bat*, she thought, shaking her head. Lifting the camera, she pointed it at herself, mimicking her father's voice as she muttered, *"Cheese,"* stretching the word in mockery of her childhood memories.

The flash detonated in her face like a miniature sun, forcing her eyes shut. When she opened them, spots danced across her vision, and for a moment, she felt disoriented, as though the room had shifted. Blinking, she laughed shakily. *That's a keeper... not.*

The camera buzzed and clicked, releasing the photograph with a soft hiss. She laid it on the table, upside down, beside the first. The minutes dragged on, tension building as she waited for it to develop, until she could finally flip it over.

The image caught her mid-expression, lips curled in a strange, toothy grimace, her eyes shut tight. Her skin was bleached by the flash, an unnatural pallor that made her look almost ghostly. She laughed, the relief flooding back, louder this time.

"Oh *god*, that... is... *horrible*," she muttered, barely hiding her embarrassment. But as she stared at the photo, something in the background caught her eye, and her laughter faded. Her breath stilled as she looked more closely.

Behind her, on the sofa, was a shadow – a figure. Not just any shadow but a man, broad-shouldered and dark, seated casually on her sofa as though he belonged there. Her heart hammered in her chest as she squinted, every nerve alert. The silhouette was indistinct, but the pose was unmistakable – one leg crossed over the other, an arm draped over the back of the sofa. Though his face was shrouded, there was an unsettling tilt to his head, an almost familiar posture, as though he were smiling.

Twisting around, her pulse thundered in her ears, and she nearly lost her balance in her rush to look. The sofa, of course, was empty, its leather smooth and undisturbed. She reached out, touching the cold leather, feeling both foolish and unsettled. The sensation did nothing to calm her nerves.

Trembling, she glanced back at the photo. The shadowy man was still there, unmoving, watching her from within the frozen frame, as if waiting for her to acknowledge him.

Without thinking, she raised the Polaroid again, aiming it at the empty sofa and pressing the shutter. The camera buzzed, clicked, and released another square of film. Heart pounding, she snatched it up, fingers cold as she watched the image slowly reveal itself.

When it was clear, she saw only the vacant sofa. Her living room was perfectly still.

Don't look into the eye, the woman's voice whispered, chilling and persistent.

"What *fucking* eye?" Karen spat, more to herself than anyone else, frustration lacing her voice.

A dark idea took root, twisting and coiling in her mind. She put the Polaroid down and crossed the room, rummaging through a drawer until she found her old digital camera. The screen blinked to life, and she felt a small surge of relief at the simple, familiar hum of technology.

She aimed it at the sofa, hesitated, then turned the lens on herself again. She pressed the shutter, the flash softer than the Polaroid's. Checking the image, she saw her own reflection smiling back, with no shadows lurking in the background.

Maybe it was just a trick of the flash, she thought, but the reassurance felt thin. Her mind drifted back to the photo with the shadowy man, too solid, too real.

Before she could stop herself, she picked up the Polaroid again, her hand trembling as she held her finger over the shutter. She wasn't really going to do it, was she? But her fingers betrayed her, and the flash exploded once more, brighter than before, leaving her stumbling back, dizzy, her legs hitting the coffee table as her head collided with something hard and unyielding.

The room spun as a grey haze settled over her vision, narrowing to a dark pinprick. The Polaroid slipped from her grasp, landing on the floor beside her as darkness enveloped her.

A few minutes after she lost consciousness, a shadow moved in the room. Rising slowly from behind the sofa, a towering man straightened, his face hidden behind the vacant eyes of a gas mask. He stood there, silent, watching her still form on the floor, his chest rising and falling with the slow, mechanical rhythm of breath concealed in shadow.

When Karen's eyes fluttered open, the first sensation that struck her was searing brightness. It cut through her awareness so intensely that she had to squeeze her eyes shut again, her head throbbing with a dull, insistent ache. Her mouth felt parched, her lips cracked, and as she tried to move her tongue, she realised something cold and unyielding was pressing against it. Her jaw was clamped around a cloth – a gag, she understood, and the realisation sent a spike of dread piercing through her mind like ice settling deep under her skin. She tried to shift, but her arms and legs wouldn't obey, held fast by something tight and unyielding. Her skin felt raw where it touched her bindings, each movement rubbing against her wrists and ankles, leaving painful, stinging trails.

Stripped to her underwear, she was tied to one of her own kitchen chairs, her limbs bound with plastic ties that bit into her skin, sending little streams of blood trickling down her arms and legs. A rising tide of panic swept through her, buzzing along her nerves like a current.

A voice, smooth and unsettlingly calm, broke through the silence. "I wouldn't try to break free if I were you," it said from somewhere beyond the blinding light that had been set up directly in front of her.

Karen squinted, straining to see past the light. All she could make out was a shadow – large, looming, and immovable as stone. Her heart thundered against her ribs. She swallowed, the gag rough against her tongue, managing a soft whimper that sounded small and strangled even to her own ears.

"If you try to break free," the man's voice continued, taking on a chilling, singsong quality, "Mother won't be too pleased." His voice fell into a low, childlike chuckle, and Karen's stomach twisted into a knot of nausea and fear.

A shift in the light signalled his approach, and then he stepped forward, his broad frame blocking the harsh glare. Her heart sank as she made out his face – or what should have been a face. He was wearing a mask: a grotesque, oversized visage marred with scratches and cracks, something monstrous pulled straight from a nightmare. In one hand, he held the Polaroid 600, the same camera that had felt so innocuous only hours earlier. In the other, he clutched something long and gleaming, reflecting the light with a deadly sheen. Recognition jolted her – a butcher's knife, the blade nicked and stained as though it had seen far too much use.

He placed the knife on her coffee table – the very table where she'd spent countless quiet evenings, a book in hand, or tapping away on her laptop. Now, that familiar space had transformed into a scene of unspeakable horror.

The masked man moved closer, and as his gloved hands hovered near her exposed thighs, Karen flinched, causing the Polaroid to slip slightly in her lap.

"*Whoa, whoa!*" he cried, his voice high and unsettlingly gentle. "Don't let it fall *off*. Mother would be *so* angry if it got damaged." His tone was mild, almost sweet, but his eyes – dark and intense behind the mask – stayed locked on her, unblinking. "It's alright. Don't worry," he cooed. "You've done nothing wrong. Mother wanted me to make sure you knew that. It's not your fault. You just... took the camera. Eventually, someone always takes it."

His massive hand reached down, retrieving the Polaroid from her lap. He raised it to his eye, pointing it at her, and Karen flinched as the flash exploded, filling her vision with a searing white light that left her momentarily dazed. She squeezed her eyes shut, shrinking back as far as her restraints would allow. The familiar buzz and whir of the Polaroid sounded disturbingly loud in the silence, followed by a soft click as the photograph slid out.

"That's going to be a good one," he snickered, dropping the photograph to the floor as if it were nothing, as if she were nothing.

He crouched down, his enormous form bending slowly, deliberately. Even crouched, he loomed over her, his head nearly level with hers. She could feel his gaze through the mask, invasive, crawling under her skin like something alive.

"We're going to play a little game," he said, his voice soft and coaxing, as though he were speaking to a child. "Just you and me and... well, let's just say Mother's always watching."

Karen tried to scream, but the gag muffled her cries into a pitiful, desperate whimper.

"Hush now. Be a good little girl," he hissed, pressing a finger to his mask's cracked, lipless mouth. "Mother doesn't like it when you make that noise. It makes the game take longer, and she doesn't like long games." He chuckled, a low, eerie sound that seemed to crawl out of his throat. "She doesn't say 'be a good little girl' to me," he continued, his tone drifting into something wistful as he stared past her, into the shadows. "She says, 'Stay in your room like a good little boy.'"

For a moment, his gaze seemed distant, lost in some dark memory, his voice dropping to a chilling whisper. "I don't like that room. It's cold and dark, and there are rats in the walls. But Mother says... Mother says..." His eyes snapped back to hers, sharp and focused. "Never mind what Mother says. What I say is that we play the game."

Karen's heartbeat pounded in her ears; each beat a harbinger of dread. *Game?* she thought, her stomach churning with fear. *What kind of game?*

His eyes darkened, a cruel gleam flickering behind the mask. "Mother calls it *selfie*." He tilted his head, as though sharing some dark joke. "There's an old belief, you see. People used to think that taking a photo stole part of your soul. I can't take your soul, so instead..." He chuckled, the sound bubbling with malice. "The idea of *selfie* is that you take parts of yourself away... and then take a photo."

Slowly, he reached behind his back, producing a small gun that looked oddly delicate in his large hand. He held it close to her face, his gloved fingers brushing against her cheek as he leaned in. "This is *Morton*," he whispered, his breath hot and damp through the mask. "Morton decides if you win or lose. And Morton is always hungry. Here's how it works, sweetheart. When I tell you which part of yourself to cut, you cut it. Then you take a picture with the Polaroid." He smiled, the expression hidden beneath the mask but revealed in the dark glint of his eyes. "Do that, and you live. Refuse... and Morton counts to three." He paused before adding distantly, "Morton doesn't like counting to three."

Karen's mind whirled, her chest heaving as panic crashed through her. Tears spilled down her cheeks, mingling with the sweat chilling her skin. The gag tasted of dust and plastic, her breaths coming in frantic, shallow gasps.

"You think you won't play the game," he said, his tone almost sympathetic. "Most people think that at first. But then they understand how hungry Morton is, and how precious life becomes." His voice softened, coaxing, like a parent urging a child. "You'll play. One way or another, you *will* play."

He picked up the knife from the coffee table, its blade gleaming, and reached towards her hand. "I'll free one of your hands so you can play. Are you right-handed or left? Doesn't matter, but Mother always says things go smoother when you use the proper hand." He cut the tie on her right wrist, and pins and needles tingled painfully as blood rushed back into her hand.

He placed the knife in her hand, and she stared at it, her knuckles whitening as she tightened her grip. The metal felt unforgiving and cold, its edge sharp against her thumb. She looked up at him, her eyes wide with terror.

"You're thinking about using it on me," he murmured, tilting his head. "They all think that. But Morton is fast. Morton is always hungry. Cheaters don't last long in Mother's game."

They locked eyes, and something inside her snapped – a cold, sickening realisation. *He's going to kill me*, she thought with chilling certainty. Whether or not she played his game, he wasn't letting her go. But if she refused, he'd end it swiftly. If she played along... if she played along, maybe she'd survive, maybe...

A flicker of the old woman's face surfaced in her mind. *Mother... it must be her*.

Karen's grip on the knife slackened slightly, and he stepped back, his posture relaxing. "Good choice," he whispered. "Now, we'll start simple. Cut off the index finger of your left hand. Once you've done that, take a picture. If you don't..." He tapped the gun against his temple. "Morton wins."

He moved behind her, pressing the cold barrel of the gun to the back of her head. His voice was a low, menacing murmur, filling her ears and mind with a terrible finality. "I'm going to count to three. If you haven't done what I asked... Morton will get his fill."

Karen's pulse hammered in her ears, every beat marking the approach of something unthinkable. Her mind scrambled, desperate for a way out, but each path ran straight into the same brick wall: the cold metal pressing against her skull and the knife in her hand, its edge biting into her sweating fingers. Her options were agonisingly clear. This man wasn't bluffing. He waited, silent and patient, holding her life in his unyielding grasp. She could almost feel the grin lurking beneath his mask as he began to count.

"One..."

Karen's gaze darted around wildly, her mind racing. Her fingers tightened around the knife. She could turn, try to stab him, make a break for it – but he was watching her too closely, ready for any flicker of resistance. Even if she struck him, Morton would still be there, waiting to end the game.

"Two..."

Her thoughts funnelled down to a single, pulsing truth: *I don't want to die.* She hadn't known how much until this moment, how fiercely she wanted to cling to life, even in this nightmare. If there was even the faintest glimmer of survival, if this horror could somehow end with her still breathing, she would take it. *Play the game*, her mind whispered. *Play, and you might live.*

With a hand that shook violently, she brought the knife to her own finger, feeling the cold steel press into her skin. Her vision blurred as tears welled up, spilling over and distorting the sight of her own trembling hand and the blade poised above it. A scream clawed at her throat, muffled by the gag, as she pressed down, feeling the knife slice through skin, muscle, and tendon.

"Three..."

Her finger came free, a burst of raw pain shooting up her arm. She slumped forward, gasping, her vision dark at the edges as agony radiated through her body. The severed digit fell onto her lap, blood pooling across her thigh. She blinked rapidly, trying to ground herself as waves of pain blurred her senses.

The masked man's laughter broke through the haze, a low, satisfied chuckle echoing through the room. "Good girl," he mocked, his voice dripping with cruel satisfaction. "Mother would be so proud."

Karen's entire body trembled as the pain tore through her, leaving her breath ragged and shallow. But her hand moved automatically, reaching for the Polaroid on the table. It felt impossibly heavy, the lens glinting coldly, like an unblinking eye trained on her suffering. She raised it, positioning it unsteadily as she forced herself to look into the viewfinder, aiming it at her pale, tear-streaked face.

"Smile," the man whispered from behind her, his breath hot against her neck, sending a chill down her spine.

She pressed the shutter.

The flash erupted, a blinding explosion of white that seared her eyes. The familiar buzz and whirr of the Polaroid followed, almost surreal in the suffocating silence, and a moment later, the photograph slid out. Her numb fingers grasped it, laying it on her lap among the bloodstains, forcing herself to look.

There she was, frozen in the frame, her face twisted in agony, blood streaking down her cheek, her eyes wide and vacant. And there, standing just behind her, loomed a shadowy figure – a dark, towering presence, face obscured by the mask's grotesque sneer, watching her with soulless, unfeeling eyes.

The man reached down, plucking the photo from her lap, holding it up to the light as if admiring a work of art. "Perfect," he whispered, his tone thick with grim satisfaction. "Mother will be pleased with this one."

He tucked the photo into his pocket, then raised the Polaroid again, tilting it at her like some twisted version of a family photographer. Karen's vision swam as the pain continued to throb; her mind barely able to process the horror unfolding around her.

"Shall we go another round?" he murmured, pressing the cold barrel of Morton against her temple.

As the countdown began again, a sickening certainty washed over her: he had no intention of letting her go. The game, this twisted game, was all he wanted, and he would keep playing it until there was nothing left.

The flash blazed one final time, casting the room into blinding light, and as the world dissolved into darkness, Karen understood with terrible clarity that the end had come.

Karen slumped forward in the chair, her head hanging low, chin resting against her bruised chest. Her hair clung to her face, matted with blood that had dried into dark streaks across her forehead. Her thoughts drifted in and out, flashes of coherence in an otherwise fractured reel of consciousness. Each snap of clarity dragged her back into the nightmare she couldn't escape.

There had been four rounds. Four brutal, soul-breaking rounds.

In the first, she'd severed her index finger. The stump still throbbed with a dull, persistent pain that pulsed even in her half-conscious state. After she had finished, he'd patted her shoulder, his voice cloying and sweet, murmuring that she'd "done such a good job." But his words held no comfort. Instead, he'd promised that each round would only get harder, even apologising in a way that felt like mockery, as though her suffering were merely a regrettable necessity.

The second round forced her to slice down her own thigh, from just above her knee to the top of her hip. She'd watched, horrified, as her hand dragged the knife along her skin, parting it in a vivid crimson line. Beneath, the raw muscle twitched as though alive. The fire of agony had ripped up her leg, searing through every exposed nerve. Her body rebelled, convulsing and vomiting even as she forced the blade onward, barely able to breathe.

By the third round, numbness had crept over her, her mind fraying as he ordered her to sever her own left hand. She had lost herself then, her voice reduced to a feeble whisper as she mouthed, "*Oh Jesus, oh Jesus,*" into the gag, over and over. Her words were barely audible, mingling with the blood that covered her face.

After each round, he made her take a photograph. He would stand back, watching with dark satisfaction as she raised the Polaroid to her face, each flash capturing a piece of her agony, one moment of degradation at a time. Now, those photographs lay scattered at her feet, each one a testament to the horror she had endured. Every time she opened her swollen, blood-crusted eyes, she was forced to see them – her own bloodied face staring back, hollow, a stranger's gaze trapped within her own.

Now, as she sagged in the chair, drifting on the edge of oblivion, she sensed him standing nearby. His shadow blocked the harsh light that had kept her disoriented, and the shift in the air made her stomach twist. The rancid odour clinging to him – an acrid blend of sweat, old grease, and something damp and rotting, like mildew – filled her nose. She realised, with a sickening pang, that he was savouring this, the twisted satisfaction clear in the way he loomed close, his breaths heavy with thrill.

Her gaze dropped to the photographs. Each one showed her further broken, another piece of herself stripped away. She could barely recognise the face staring back from those images – her cheeks were swollen, her mouth slack, her teeth loosened, some barely held in place. But it was the emptiness in her eyes that made her heart stammer. She no longer recognised herself. She was becoming... something else, something hollow.

"We're almost done," he murmured, his voice soft but thick with anticipation. He knelt before her, his shadow draping across her battered face as he leaned closer. "Mother will be so proud of you, you know. Just a couple more rounds, and then... freedom."

A whimper slipped from her cracked lips, low and barely audible. Her entire body ached; her bones weighed down by relentless pain. Her left hand was a vacant throb, the raw stump radiating waves of agony through her. She tried to shake her head, but the movement was feeble, her consciousness flickering like a dim flame.

He tilted his head, studying her as though listening to some distant voice only he could hear. Silence gathered around them, heavy as oil, smothering the room. After what felt like an eternity, he finally spoke.

"I'll remove the gag now, so you can talk," he said, his voice almost gentle but edged with malice. "But if you scream..." He tapped the cold barrel of the gun – Morton – against her temple, a silent warning pressing into her skin.

Slowly, he reached forward, his rough fingers brushing her swollen mouth as he pulled the gag down. Pain flared in her jaw, and her teeth clung weakly to her gums. A trickle of blood pooled on her lips as she coughed, the wet taste filling her mouth. Four teeth slipped free, clattering onto the floor, rolling into the scattered photographs, smearing them with fresh spatters of blood.

"*No! No!*" he shrieked suddenly, his voice twisting into a pitch of panic as he lunged for the photographs, his hands frantic as he wiped the blood from them. "Mother's going to be so cross with you. So *cross*..."

Karen watched, her throat raw, her voice little more than a rasp. "Please..." The word was a whisper, her desperation bleeding through.

He glanced up, his head tilting like a curious animal. "What's that?"

"Please... no more." Her voice cracked, barely more than a breath, each syllable coated in blood and fear.

Straightening, he tapped Morton against his palm thoughtfully. "I don't understand. You girls love games. Love taking selfies." His voice took on a singsong quality, mocking, taunting. "Why are you saying 'no more'? Only a couple more rounds, and then... you're free."

But she knew better now. She could see it in the gleam of his eyes, glinting from behind the mask. There was no end to this game, no freedom waiting for her. Her life had been reduced to this sequence of agonising moments, captured forever in those blood-streaked photos. She would die here, in the stillness of her own flat, a silence no one would think to break.

"I can't," she whispered, her voice fading, a fragile thread in the darkness.

He rose to his full height, and she lifted her head, summoning every ounce of strength to meet the cold, dead eyes of his mask.

"Why can't you understand?" Her voice cracked with desperation, her words trembling. "I've done everything. Why isn't that enough?"

He took a step back, his tone soft, almost reverent. "Because Mother told me which rounds to play. She'll know if I skip them. She'll know... by the photos." His voice grew sharper, dripping with cruelty. "She said, 'Make sure that prissy little thing doesn't look so pretty anymore. Don't stop until she's unrecognisable.' And that's exactly what we'll do. The next round."

With deliberate slowness, he picked up the knife and slipped it into her hand. Her fingers curled around it instinctively, though the pain that radiated up her arm was nearly unbearable. He leaned in, his breath warm and sickly as he whispered, "Mother says you have to choose which part you don't like. So... which one will it be?"

Horror washed over her, thick and cold, as his meaning became clear. Her chest heaved, a shattered sob rising in her throat. "*No,*" she gasped. "*Please*... don't make me..."

The man raised Morton, his finger grazing the trigger. "Are you giving up?" His voice was a low, predatory growl. "Morton thinks you are." The click of the hammer pulling back filled her ears, slicing through her like a blade.

"I don't... want to... *die*," she choked out, the words barely forming through her cracked, bloodied lips.

He pressed the gun between her eyes, the cold metal digging into her bruised skin. "Then play the game."

With chilling finality, he forced the gag back into her mouth, tightening it until her screams were reduced to strangled sobs. He guided her trembling hand to her chest, pressing the knife against the curve of her right breast, the blade cold and merciless.

Tears poured down her face as she pressed the knife to her skin, the agony piercing, blinding, flaring through her every nerve. She screamed into the gag, each muffled cry a testament to the horror that had become her reality.

He watched, his eyes gleaming from behind the mask, his breaths shallow, his presence vibrating with a sick, hungry thrill. "Sometimes," he murmured, voice thick with dark reverence, "the beautiful lie we call life can hide the truth of death... so Mother says."

As the flash of the Polaroid burst through the room one last time, Karen knew she'd been emptied, lost. All that remained were scattered photographs, fragments of a shattered soul, each one a piece of her agony, forever caught in the eye of that cursed lens.

In the small shop on Main Street of Fallen Ridge, filled with old, second-hand items, the woman hobbled across the floor, each step slow and deliberate. Her bones creaked and cracked with every movement, as though she were some ancient machine, long past its prime but grinding forward out of sheer, stubborn will. When she reached her rickety chair, it groaned along with her as she lowered herself into it, both woman and chair settling into place with a chorus of pops and sighs. Her cloudy eyes drifted to the shelf she'd come from, where, nestled among the dust and decay, sat the Polaroid 600.

The camera looked innocuous – an ordinary relic from another time, just worn enough to be unremarkable. Positioned towards the back of the shelf, it lingered, barely visible, yet tantalising enough to catch the eye of any curious passer-by. Eventually, someone always noticed it.

With a satisfied sigh, she leaned back, her gaze shifting to the counter in front of her. Beneath it, hidden from wandering eyes, lay her private trove – a stack of Polaroid photos, each one capturing a moment of agony, each frame a small window into the suffering her boy had crafted, preserved forever in film. Her gnarled fingers trembled slightly as she lifted the stack, thumbing through the most recent additions. Five photos all from last night's game.

It had been a decent showing. Not the longest her boy had ever managed, but respectable. The first photo had disappointed her – a mere severed finger, its pale stump stark against the girl's shocked expression. But by the second photo, her boy had found his rhythm, cutting deeper, each image more gruesome than the last. And the girl – she'd been a resilient one. Most broke by the third round, begging for release, but this one had clung to life, her defiance making each cut, each tear, more exquisite. A minor masterpiece, really.

The woman's eyes lingered over each photo, savouring the details one by one. A mangled hand, a gaping wound tracing the girl's thigh, her swollen face streaked with tears and blood, bruised skin giving way to shattered bone. The last photograph showed her head slumped forward, her skin pale as wax, drained of life. Her son had taken one last picture, capturing her in that quiet, final surrender. There was a beauty to it, in its own way.

She had watched the entire ordeal unfold through the camera's eye, its cold, unfeeling lens documenting each scream, every whimper, every drop of blood. She leaned back; her twisted satisfaction settling in as she imagined the girl's last moments, her suffering immortalised on film. Yes, her boy had done well.

FALLEN RIDGE

The Polaroid camera had been with them from the beginning, back when her husband was still alive. They'd bought it as newlyweds, an impulsive little luxury, when owning such a camera felt thrilling. But the game had come later, sprouting from a dark inspiration, a passing idea that had festered and grown into an obsession. They had begun with drifters – those who wandered in unnoticed, people no one would miss. A few cuts here, a few bruises there, each photograph a small thrill, an intimacy unlike any other, capturing life and death side by side in a single frame.

Her gaze grew distant, drifting to the cracked ceiling as old memories flickered to life. She and her husband had found joy in the quiet terror of others, a thrill that bound them together, each image a testament to the strange communion of blood and loyalty. Blood had soaked into this floor, staining the wood, marking the shop with memories no one could erase. She'd felt alive then, more alive than ever before, with the taste of life and death mingling in the air like iron on her tongue. And when her husband passed, an empty hunger gnawed within her – a hollow grief that consumed, devouring her until only this "game" could fill the void. Her son had inherited the duty, his loyalty and obedience forged by blood and the twisted legacy left by his father.

A faint creak sounded behind her, snapping her back to the present. The door to the small, shadowed room at the back of the shop had opened a crack, a sliver of light spilling through. The old woman didn't turn. She didn't need to. She knew who stood there, lingering in the darkness like a ghost awaiting permission to step forward.

"Close the door," she rasped, her voice a brittle croak, thick with age. Her gaze remained fixed on the Polaroid; her expression unchanging. "Stay in your room like a good little boy."

For a moment, silence enveloped them, thick and stifling as the dust blanketing the shop. Then, a quiet, obedient murmur drifted from the darkness: "Yes, Mother."

The door creaked shut, the latch clicking softly, leaving the shop steeped in silence once more. Alone, she hunched over the stack of Polaroids, each image a stark reminder of the legacy she'd built. Her fingers brushed the cool, smooth surface of the Polaroid 600, a relic from another time yet essential to her work. She left it there on the shelf, just as she always did, waiting.

Because eventually, someone would come. Someone would see it, nestled among the clutter, tucked away but irresistible. They would pick it up, feel its weight, drawn to its charm, its quaint promise of nostalgia. And, as always, they would think themselves lucky to have found such a prize.

A slow smile crept across her face, splitting her dry, cracked lips, as she settled back into her chair. There was always someone who couldn't resist.

And, as always, the game would begin again.

CHAPTER SEVEN

THE WATCHER IN THE WALL

MARA STONE WAS TOUGH, as tough as an old dog's bone left gnawed and weathered. Growing up on the grimmest streets of the city, she'd witnessed her fair share of strange, unsettling things. She'd lived in her share of rat-infested flats, the kind where locks never truly locked, and neighbours spoke too loudly of matters better left unsaid. But this new place in Fallen Ridge... this one was different. Not the usual damp, drafty sort of different, but the kind that clung to you like a splinter embedded under the skin, prickling and festering.

The building was old – ancient, really, by the Ridge standards. Its walls were thick, close as a crypt, damp and seeping with age, as though exhaling the memory of lives long past. Her landlord had called it *full of character*. That was his phrasing. *Full of character*. But he'd failed to mention that some of those characters hadn't moved on.

The unease started small, as these things do. A chill settled in her bedroom, raising the fine hairs on her arms, a cold that stubbornly held its ground even in the smothering heat of a

February night. "It's nothing," she muttered to herself in the darkness, her voice swallowed by shadows stretching thick and sticky across the floorboards. *Probably just a bad circuit*, she reasoned. *Perhaps the old wiring was shoddy*. But every night, at precisely 3:13, the cold would crawl over her, insidious and relentless, seeping into her bones like venom.

Then the dreams began.

They arrived quiet as dusk, shadow slipping down walls. Each night she'd find herself in a vast black space, frigid as a grave. She could hear whispers, low and indistinct, like wind rustling dry leaves, speaking words she couldn't grasp. Shapes moved around her, flickering in awkward, unnatural jerks. And always, at her feet, lay the symbol. Every dream, it would appear: a blood-red marking on the floor, twisting and pulsing, almost alive. It throbbed beneath her feet like the heartbeat of something ancient and unspeakable.

Each morning she'd awake feeling the weight of its presence in her room. She didn't need to look. She knew it was there, hanging just beyond her bed, dense and watchful.

After two weeks of these night terrors, she reached her limit. Though she hadn't wanted to, Mara finally went to her neighbours, desperate for answers. Mrs. Galbraith, the old woman with hair like grey cobwebs who lived across the hall, greeted her without a blink.

"Oh, the Watcher," Mrs. Galbraith murmured, her voice brittle and dry as paper cracking in the heat. Her clouded eyes shone with something Mara chose not to understand. "That old shadow's been here long before you, love. Best to ignore it. It doesn't like to be seen."

Another neighbour, a quiet man with haunted eyes and hands that trembled as he spoke, shook his head when Mara brought it up. "Don't search for it," he whispered, voice hollow. "The Watcher doesn't take kindly to being looked at. Some things simply... *are*. We don't question them."

Moving out crossed Mara's mind. She even packed a few boxes. But leaving would mean admitting fear, and Mara Stone wasn't one to scare easily. So she stayed, trying to live as though the Watcher weren't real. But like smoke from a hidden fire, it permeated every corner of her life. She felt it in the ghostly breath that skimmed the back of her neck while she showered, in the faint, scratching noises within the walls as she lay in bed, in the faint flickers of shadow at the edges of her vision.

And then, one night, it did more than watch.

She woke at 3:13, her skin crawling, her breath fogging in the chill. But this time, she wasn't alone. At the foot of her bed loomed a figure, blacker than the darkest night, its form shifting like oil on water. Its eyes were pits of emptiness, consuming the surrounding light. It leaned forward, a faceless presence, and whispered in a voice that crackled and grated like static: "I am bound to you, Mara. I am bound to this place. You cannot rid yourself of me."

She jerked back, her heart hammering so loud it drowned out her thoughts. The creature lingered, hovering over her like the ghost of a dying breath, and she understood then that light was no remedy for this darkness. It wasn't just inside her flat. It had burrowed into her, rooted deep, festering.

The next day, bleary-eyed and drained, Mara dragged herself to the library. She spent hours amongst the dust and decay of old books, searching for anything that might hold an answer, a remedy for what plagued her. Finally, she found a weathered tome on the occult, its pages fragile with age. It spoke of entities tied to places, to bricks and mortar, feeding on fear, thriving on human terror.

That night, she returned to her flat with a trembling sense of resolve. Armed with a single candle, she perched cross-legged on her bed, clutching it as though it held the key to her survival. As the clock ticked toward 3:13, she chanted, her voice barely a whisper. "You have no power over me. I deny you. I banish you."

The room fell silent, a silence so thick it pressed against her eardrums. The candle flame flickered, casting warped shadows across the walls. And then the Watcher slipped from the darkness, moving like a serpent. It loomed over her, growing until it filled her vision, its breath chilling her to her core.

"Words cannot save you," it sneered, its voice dripping with malice. "I was here long before you, long before your kind crawled out of the darkness."

The shadows thickened, spreading across the walls like a blight. Mara's voice wavered as she chanted, louder now, her desperation rising. "You don't own me. *I banish you!*"

The creature chuckled, a low, mocking sound that twisted her insides. Its hand, black as void, hovered just over her heart, and the coldness there stabbed at her chest.

"You are mine," it hissed. "You welcomed me in."

Her voice faltered, terror closing off her throat. She felt it pressing into her thoughts, twisting her fear like a blade. She was trapped, helpless, the creature's darkness seeping into her, creeping through her veins. Just as she was on the edge of surrender, a pale light of dawn crept through the window. The shadow recoiled, shrinking back with a hiss.

And then it was gone, leaving Mara gasping in the dim light of morning.

But she knew this was only a reprieve. The creature was bound to her, tethered to the walls, waiting for her guard to slip. Days turned to nights, and though its presence faded with each sunrise, she knew it had not gone far.

One night, exhausted beyond words, she lay down, her body heavy, her breath shallow, hoping for peace in sleep. But as darkness closed in, a cold settled over her, final and unyielding, like a shroud draped over her heart.

Her eyes snapped open, but she was paralysed, her body unresponsive, frozen. She tried to scream, to even twitch a finger, but she was rooted in place, trapped. In that silence, she felt it – something creeping beneath her skin, oozing into her veins, thick and suffocating, spreading slowly, inch by inch. The Watcher was inside her now, filling the hollow places, binding itself to her soul.

A voice that was not hers, deep and seething, wove itself through Mara's mind. You invited me in, it whispered, coiling around her thoughts with quiet triumph. This body... will do just fine.

Mara's mind staggered under the weight of it, her terror clawing upward, tightening in her throat as she struggled to reclaim control. She fought against the suffocating presence, her every cell straining, every instinct screaming to move, to breathe, to survive. But her limbs lay rigid, her mouth sealed as though bound. She could feel the Watcher rooting itself deeper, threading into her thoughts, smothering her in waves of unnatural cold that sapped every trace of warmth, draining her essence.

In the dark corners of her mind, Mara resisted. A sick realisation crept over her: there was only one way out. The Watcher was feeding on her life, drawing from her, but if she could starve it – if she could deny it, the life it sought...

Not... like... this! The thought forced itself through her mind, a raw defiance burning strong and silent. She centred herself on the rhythm of her heartbeat, each beat weaker than the last, a metronome winding down. Mara pulled her focus inward, rejecting the Watcher's snarled whispers, shunning the oppressive cold as she willed her heart to slow. She'd sever its hold, cut off its life source.

But the Watcher sensed her intent and retaliated with a violent fury. A searing pain detonated in her skull, and her vision flooded with shapes and colours that defied reason. Pulsing shadows shot through with blistering red. It plunged deeper into her mind, filling her thoughts with twisted, impossible images – memories of horrors that only it had known, images that clawed at her sanity. Mara's senses unravelled, and somewhere in the blackened recesses, she heard the desperate cries of others. They were the trapped voices of those before her, echoes of lost souls, their screams a cacophony that stretched on and on through shadowed corridors without end.

Her own silent scream joined theirs, an agonised cry trapped within her mind as the Watcher's force surged, trying to consume her whole. Yet she clung to the last frail remnants of her will, though they slipped from her like dry sand through desperate fingers.

Then... it was over. Her body lay still, lips parted slightly, her eyes glassy and vacant, emptied of Mara's spark. The Watcher had taken what it desired. It had no interest in the body – only the life it had drained from it.

Hours later, her landlord, Hal – a burly, gruff man who prided himself on his unshakeable nerves – came to her flat, knocking loudly. When there was no answer, he entered, muttering her name as he looked around. She was sitting on the edge of her bed as though waiting, her head tilted, her eyes wide and unseeing. A chill prickled the back of his neck as he stepped closer, waving a cautious hand in front of her face. She didn't respond, and he leaned in, studying her expression.

Mara's eyes stared straight ahead, sunken and hollow, ringed in bruised darkness that gave her the look of something decayed from the inside. Her mouth hung slightly open, a look of silent dread. Her skin looked thin, stretched, barely clinging to the bones beneath, as if there hadn't been enough life left to fill it.

"*Jesus,*" he whispered, backing away, his heartbeat a hammer in his chest. The air had thickened around him, a weight pressing down, something unseen and wrong. He stumbled back, refusing to turn his back on her, her lifeless eyes seeming to track him as he fumbled his way to the door.

Once outside, he leaned against the wall, breathing heavily, steadying himself before he called the Sheriff. Yet even as he dialled, the impression of her empty gaze lingered, etched into his mind.

But he hadn't seen what happened next.

Inside the apartment, as the early morning shadows stretched and pooled, Mara's body remained motionless. Yet behind her, a darkness gathered, inky and restless, spreading across the wall like spilled ink. The darkness twisted, morphing into a crude imitation of her form – a face, a body, eyes wide and gleaming with a hunger that wasn't hers. Mara's lips curled into a grin that no one could witness.

The shade that had once been Mara lingered there, silent and watchful, waiting. It would bide its time. Shadows thickened in the room, pressing against the silence, her shape lingering, watching, until another tenant came along and dared to open the door.

Chapter Eight

THE WELL OF REGRETS

IN THE FORGOTTEN OUTSKIRTS of Fallen Ridge, hidden down an overgrown lane choked with thorn bushes and wild ivy, sat the old White farmhouse. Time had not been kind to it. Once-white paint flaked away like old parchment, exposing timber as grey and warped as sun-bleached driftwood. Broken glass caught the fading light like dead eyes in the shattered windows, and the roof sagged under years of relentless winters and harsh summers. The air around the house was thick with the presence of ancient neglect, a silence broken only by the whispering breeze and the mournful creak of drooping willows that seemed to claw at the walls, as if to pry open the secrets hidden within.

The townsfolk spun their tales. They called the farmhouse haunted, claimed strange noises echoed through the night, and swore that if the wind carried right, you could catch the faint murmur of voices. But no one dared venture near, for Fallen Ridge was a place of quiet, where whispers spread like fire, and no one wanted to stoke the flames with stories of the "cursed" White house. Especially since old Agnes White still lived there, veiled from prying eyes, a shadow within a ghostly home.

Agnes, now as frail and spectral as the home itself, wandered the empty rooms like a phantom of the past. Her hands, once quick, trembled with age, her fingers knobbed and thin as winter branches. Her hair, wispy and colourless as smoke, framed eyes once bright but now clouded, dulled by a lifetime's regrets. For years, she'd kept to herself, turning away from the well-meaning neighbours who occasionally left casseroles on her porch. She had no need for kindness; she bore a burden heavier than sympathy could lighten, a burden rooted in a single night she tried, and failed, to forget.

Tonight marked the anniversary of that night – the night Harold, her husband, had vanished into the well behind their home. The night she had watched him tumble; his scream swallowed by darkness. She hadn't meant for it to happen – or perhaps, in a truth she dared not fully admit, she had. Harold was a hard man, his voice sharp and bitter as a broken bottle, his temper as volatile as the storm that had howled that evening. He drank, he raged, and when thwarted, his fists struck out.

The memory of that storm clawed at her mind. Rain had lashed against the windows, and thunder had roared as if the heavens themselves shared her fury. When he raised his hand that night, something in her snapped. She gave a single, forceful shove, and he staggered back, teetering on the edge of the well. His face – a blend of shock and fear – twisted into a scream as he fell. She hadn't moved, hadn't reached to save him; she had simply listened as his cry faded, replaced by the wet, hollow silence the well held like a secret.

Since that night, Agnes's life had become a prison. The silence she once sought had become a cage, smothering her. In the deepest hours of night, she sometimes thought she heard him – the drip of water, a faint echo carrying her name: *Agnes... Agnes... why?* But it was her mind, she told herself. Her guilt, whispering back at her from the shadows.

As the years passed, the world around her moved on, and Harold's disappearance became yet another Fallen Ridge mystery – a hushed story told over bonfires and church socials, a riddle with no answer. But as her body weakened and her mind grew brittle, Agnes found herself drawn back to that night, as if the well itself beckoned, refusing to let her forget.

Tonight, as she sat by the dying fire, the storm gathered again, as it had all those years ago. Wind howled through the trees, their branches scratching at the windows like skeletal hands, and rain lashed against the glass, each droplet a relentless knock. Shadows danced on the walls, twisting and crawling up like blackened ivy. Agnes drew her quilt tightly around her shoulders, but the warmth did little to stave off the chill creeping through her bones.

She closed her eyes, hoping to quiet the memories, but the storm only intensified the sounds in her mind – the wind, the rain, and the slow, rhythmic drip of water she thought she'd forgotten. Then, through the din, she heard it.

Agnes...

The voice slipped into her mind like ice water, chilling her to her core. Her eyes snapped open, her heart hammering. She told herself it was the wind, the creak of the old house, perhaps the pipes groaning with age—but her instincts whispered otherwise.

Agnes...

The voice grew louder, sharper, and she recognised it with a terror that turned her blood cold. She would never forget that voice.

"Harold," she breathed, barely a whisper, her hands clutching the armrests, their wood rough and unforgiving under her fingers. She strained to hear, hoping the sound would vanish, but then she heard it again – footsteps, slow and deliberate, echoing from the back door. Dread took root as she watched dark, damp footprints bloom across the floor, each one soaking into the boards like ink. They traced a path from the back door toward her.

With a crack of thunder, a figure took shape in the doorway, emerging from the shadows with a slow, unnatural grace. Harold's bloated, waterlogged form drifted towards her, his clothes dripping, his face pale and twisted. His hollow eyes—empty, dark voids—locked onto her, and a sickly, rotting stench filled the room.

"Agnes," he rasped, his voice thick and guttural, as though he were still drowning. "Why?"

Agnes's heart thundered in her chest; her throat clenched tight with terror. She could not move, could not scream. She could only watch as Harold's ghost drew closer, leaving a trail of wet decay in his wake, chilling the room until her breath fogged the air.

Summoning the last fragments of courage, Agnes rose to her feet, her body stiff and trembling. "Harold," she whispered, her voice barely audible. "I – I had no choice. It was you or me."

The spectre paused, his lips curling into a ghastly, mocking smile. "But you stayed, didn't you, Agnes?" His voice grated like stone against iron. "You lived here, alone... and listened to me... every... *night*."

Tears burned her eyes, and her knees threatened to buckle. She wanted to run, to flee from the horrors her mind had buried, but she stood rooted, paralysed by years of silence, by guilt that bound her like chains. The room darkened as he loomed closer, the rot of his presence seeping into her lungs, suffocating her.

"*Please*," she whimpered, her voice cracked and fragile. But Harold stepped forward, his gaze fixed, his dripping hands reaching out.

The floor under her feet felt sodden as water spread, staining her nightdress and soaking into the quilt she clung to as though it might protect her. "You should have joined me, Agnes," he hissed, his fingers brushing her cheek. The touch sent a shiver deep into her marrow. "You belong there too."

With a surge of primal fear, Agnes wrenched herself free, stumbling towards the door. She burst outside into the raging storm, rain stinging her face as wind tore at her thin frame. Her heart pounded as she made her way around the house, her feet sinking into mud as she approached the well, her body pulled towards its depths by a morbid gravity.

Lightning fractured the sky, casting the well in a harsh, unnatural light, transforming it into a dark maw that seemed to breathe. She gripped the well's crumbling stones, her heart racing, her skin cold and clammy. She stared into the darkness below, her mind filling with visions of the stagnant water, black as the secrets she had buried.

"I'm sorry," she whispered into the storm, her tears mingling with the rain. "I never meant..." But her voice faltered, smothered by the whisper rising from the well's depths: *Come home, Agnes. Come home...*

Shuddering, she staggered back, her heart a drumbeat of raw terror. Yet even as she stepped away, she felt the earth shift beneath her, as though the well itself sought to draw her in.

In a moment of clarity, she understood she had never escaped. She had stayed bound to this place, shackled to the memory, tethered to the shadows of her own guilt. The well had claimed a piece of her, a part she would never retrieve.

Come home, it murmured, that relentless whisper curling through the storm, tugging at her soul. She felt herself teetering on the edge, her will slipping away, her resolve draining. But as her foot hovered over the abyss, a spark of defiance flickered within her, faint but determined.

"No," she murmured, her voice thin but resolute. "I survived. And I will not let *you* take me."

In the stillness that followed, the storm seemed to hold its breath. She felt the voice fade, the grip of the darkness loosened, leaving only silence. With trembling hands, Agnes stumbled back from the well, her breath ragged as she lost her footing and came down hard against the ground, rapping her head hard against a rock.

The first light of dawn crept over Fallen Ridge, casting a dull, grey pallor over the farmhouse. The storm had departed, leaving behind a dense, damp silence, as though it had drained every sound from the world along with the night. Mist clung low to the ground, and the air was thick with the earthy scent of rain-soaked soil, heavy and lingering like a memory.

Sheriff Dalton guided his police car carefully along the winding, muddy road, the wheels struggling against the sodden earth as they edged closer to the old White farmhouse. He was a man with a face weathered by years of hard-won insight, his gaze sharp yet shadowed, every line a testament to the secrets he'd encountered but had never shared. Dalton had known Agnes White for as long as he could remember – she'd been a part of the Ridge for decades, like the hills and trees, and had outlasted both the gossip and the sympathy that came her way. She was the solitary woman at the edge of town, cloaked in tragedy, yet unreachable by those who meant to help her.

Stepping out of the car, Dalton adjusted his hat and cast a long look at the house. It loomed before him, spectral in the dawn light, as though the storm had stripped away whatever frail vitality remained. The walls were bleached and peeling, worn down to a prison of shadows that seemed to cling to the timber, hiding something darker within. A chill slithered up his spine, filling him with an old, nameless dread. It was as if the house itself held on to sorrow, some residue of grief and fear that refused to fade, no matter how many years passed.

He moved cautiously around the side of the house, his boots sinking into the mud with every step. That's when he saw her. Agnes, lying beside the well, her frail body curled inwards, her limbs tangled as if resisting the stiff embrace of the earth. She looked brittle, a leaf clinging to life long after its time. Dalton's heart clenched, and he hurried to her side, half-expecting the worst. But as he knelt beside her, he noticed the faint rise and fall of her chest, her breaths shallow but present, each one clinging to life as tenuously as she herself did.

"Agnes?" he whispered, placing a gentle hand on her shoulder. Her eyelids fluttered, and for a moment, her gaze was wild, unseeing, her eyes clouded with something he couldn't name. She looked right through him, as if lost in some shadowed memory, caught between here and a place much darker.

"It's me, Tom," he said, his voice a low, calming murmur. "You're safe now. The storm's over."

She blinked, her gaze slowly focusing, and recognition dawned in her eyes, dispelling some shadows. "Sheriff," she murmured, her voice so faint he had to lean in to catch it. "He... he was here. Harold..."

Dalton's jaw tightened as he absorbed her words. He'd heard the rumours, the tales whispered around town about Harold's disappearance on a night much like this one. Ghost stories, people had called them – fragments of mystery woven into the fabric of Fallen Ridge. But now, as he met Agnes's haunted gaze, a shiver of doubt threaded through his mind, unsettling his long-held scepticism.

"Come on," he whispered, helping her to her feet. She was light, her bones sharp beneath her thin frame, and she leaned heavily on him, her steps faltering as they made their way back towards the house. The closer they came, the more Dalton felt the house's oppressive atmosphere; he couldn't shake the feeling of being watched, of eyes hidden in every shadow, lingering just out of sight.

Inside, the air was thick with a musty, sour smell, a scent that seemed to rise from the very walls, as though the wood itself had soaked up years of grief and neglect. He settled Agnes into her chair by the fireplace, though the hearth was cold, the last of the ashes long since extinguished. She gripped the edges of an old quilt, her knuckles pale as bone, her gaze fixed on the empty hearth as though it still held the flicker of last night's fire, still whispered with the shadows that had danced there.

"Agnes," Dalton spoke quietly, kneeling beside her to catch her gaze. "Tell me what happened."

She didn't respond at first, her eyes distant, drifting through memories he couldn't see. When she finally spoke, her voice was barely a whisper, brittle as winter frost.

"He came back," she murmured, her voice raw with dread. Her hands tightened on the quilt, as though it were the only thing keeping her grounded. "After all these years... he came back. He... he wants me to go with him. To join him."

Tom's face remained calm, though he felt a hollow ache of unease settle in his chest. He'd seen many things over the years, had heard countless stories of grief, of ghosts haunting those who couldn't let them go. But there was something about the look in her eyes – a haunted vacancy that made him feel, for a moment, as though he too could sense Harold's presence. It wasn't the first time Tom Dalton had felt a presence of some-*thing*.

He paused, choosing his words carefully. "Agnes... whatever happened that night, perhaps it's time you spoke to someone. A doctor, maybe. Someone who might help."

Her gaze sharpened slightly, and she shook her head, a bitter smile flickering at the corners of her mouth. "No doctor can mend this, Sheriff," she said, her voice laced with a sorrow that cut through him like a blade. "I made my peace long ago, if such a thing even exists. Now, I have only to endure it."

Dalton studied her, his eyes filled with a quiet compassion that he rarely showed. He wanted to tell her she wasn't alone, that she didn't need to carry this weight by herself, but he knew words were useless here, hollow reassurances against a lifetime of regret.

"If you ever need anything, Agnes," he said softly, "you know where I am."

She didn't reply, her gaze still locked on the empty fireplace, and he understood it as a dismissal. Rising, he glanced around one last time, the silence pressing against him like a suffocating shroud. As he stepped back outside, he turned to look at the well, its stone rim glistening with a few last drops of rainwater, the morning light casting strange shadows that clung to its edges. A chill threaded down his spine, and he quickened his steps, feeling a powerful urge to leave this place behind.

Inside, Agnes sat in the quiet, the emptiness around her settling like dust. She closed her eyes, hoping to find relief in the darkness, but the silence only magnified the memory of Harold's empty gaze, the void in his eyes that had swallowed all light. She opened her eyes again, but the shadows remained, clinging to the corners of the room, filling it with a soft hum that pulsed, rising and falling in time with her breaths.

As the sun rose, thin beams of light crept through the window, casting faint patches of warmth across the floor. She felt a sliver of peace – a fragile, temporary reprieve – but deep within, she knew it would not last. The well's darkness lingered, waiting, its depths bound to hers so she could neither escape nor ignore.

And as she sat in that silence, alone in the house that had become both her prison and her penance, a faint, mocking whisper rose from the shadows, curling up from the floorboards like smoke, filling the room with a chilling echo.

Come home, Agnes... come home...

She closed her eyes, her hands clutching the quilt tighter, and for the first time in years, a faint, bitter smile tugged at her lips. Perhaps, after all, she would.

Chapter Nine

THE SHADOWS

IN FALLEN RIDGE, THERE'S a saying whispered in back rooms and shadowed doorways: "If you've got a problem, take it to Sheriff Dalton – but only if you're prepared to pay the price." No one dared speak too plainly about that "price," but they all knew it wasn't something to be taken lightly. Sheriff Tom Dalton was the kind of man who could freeze a person to the bone with just a look, his gaze as sharp and unyielding as a drawn blade. Even on his best days, folks stepped off the pavement to avoid passing too close.

Dalton was a giant of a man, towering at six foot six, weighing close to seventeen stone, with hands that looked as though they'd been carved from iron. His stare carried the weight of a confession, a force that could make you feel your own sins rise to the surface, as if you'd already admitted every wrong you'd ever committed. Standing under his gaze was like standing in judgment.

As dusk settled over Fallen Ridge, Dalton walked the length of the main street, his heavy steps marking time against the cracked pavement. The air was thick, smelling of decay, like something rotting beneath the earth's surface, a stench that rose with the evening wind, carrying an age-old rot that had lingered for years. The Ridge was a place that felt buried from the world, a secret held too close, too long.

Dalton knew that smell well. He'd worn the sheriff's badge for fourteen years, and the town had never changed; its secrets seemed to fester beneath the dusty soil, hidden but never forgotten. That slow, creeping rot didn't trouble him – nothing much did.

When people in Fallen Ridge found themselves in trouble, they went to Dalton. Sometimes he'd resolve it with a quiet word and a hard look that left them unable to sleep that night. Other times, his solutions lingered, bitter and unsettling, the kind that left a man turning over memories with an unpleasant taste in his mouth. People knew better than to ask questions. Some said that when Dalton took over from old Sheriff Boone, stray dogs disappeared from the streets. Others whispered about things much darker. But Dalton wasn't the sort of man who tolerated loose ends; he made things disappear when they needed to vanish.

And as for payment? Tom Dalton was the kind of man who collected favours in a currency more binding than money. He had a way of taking what he wanted when he wanted it, and the people of Fallen Ridge had long since learned there was no saying no.

People in Fallen Ridge had a way of avoiding the Dalton family, as if staying silent about them could somehow keep their shadows from seeping into everyday life. There was a quiet superstition in town: you didn't speak of the Daltons, didn't ask questions, didn't linger too long near their land. You kept your head down, stayed polite, and hoped whatever curse seemed to cling to them wouldn't take root elsewhere. No one could have foreseen that the wiry, intense boy with bruised knuckles and haunted eyes would grow into the man they'd all come to fear.

Tom Dalton grew up on the edge of town, in a house that crouched low in a field, dark and rotting, like something festering in the earth. The paint had long since flaked away, leaving the walls exposed, grey and brittle, as if bleached by sorrow. It was a house that creaked in the wind, its timbers bending and whispering, as though something restless lay within. Some people chalked it up to the place simply being old; others spoke in hushed tones of something darker, something unspeakable.

Inside, the house was silent – oppressively so. Tom's mother, Ruth Dalton, wore grief in her very bones, her face sharp enough to cut glass and her eyes as pale and hard as a winter morning. Once, they said, Ruth had been a beauty, but whatever light she'd carried had gone out long ago. She never laughed, never even smiled. Only once had Tom heard her laugh, late one night behind her bedroom door—a thin, choked sound that was a more strangled gasp than a laugh, laced with something that might have been fear. Tom lay awake, his heart pounding, certain she wasn't alone, though no other voice drifted from that room.

Tom's younger brother, Bobby, had always been a fragile, anxious boy. He moved with a wary lightness, his eyes flickering from one shadow to the next, as if something might leap from the darkness at any moment. His thin frame and nervous hands made him look as though he might blow away with a powerful gust, an ever-present tension as if bracing for some invisible blow. Bobby kept to himself, rarely playing with other children, rarely stepping outside the safety of the house. There was a fear in him that Tom could never quite understand – a fear of things hidden, things lurking in the quiet corners of the world.

One evening, Bobby approached Tom, his face pale, his small hands twisting anxiously in his shirt. "Mum says there's something in the basement," he whispered, barely loud enough to hear, his eyes wide and fixed on Tom as if seeking reassurance.

Tom forced a scoff, though he felt a chill ripple through him. "There's nothing down there, Bobby. Just old boxes and spiders," he muttered, trying to sound dismissive, but the tightness in his chest betrayed him.

Bobby wouldn't relent. "No, Tom," he insisted, his voice trembling, "I hear it... sometimes, at night... it whispers my name."

The night clung to Tom's skin like a fevered mist, thick and suffocating, heavy with heat and humidity. The air pressed in around him, so dense that breathing felt like trying to swallow something thick and sweet. Tom lay in bed, sheets tangled around his legs, staring at the ceiling. Sleep wouldn't come. Outside, the crickets' shrill chorus rose, a relentless, pulsing sound that made his head throb. His mind drifted to Bobby, alone down in the basement, and with it came a familiar mix of irritation and something else – something closer to concern. Bobby always needed something: a glass of water, a dim light, a few soft words to banish his fear of shadows.

But tonight, something felt different.

A new sound emerged, so faint that Tom wasn't sure he'd heard it at all – a whimper, soft and desperate, like a trapped animal struggling in its last moments.

He froze, tension locking his muscles. It was Bobby's whimper. He'd heard it drift up from the basement before, but this time, it held a rawness, a kind of pleading, as if each cry clawed its way up, gasping for air. The sound twisted inside his head, crawling under his skin, until he stood, his body moving on instinct.

The floorboards creaked underfoot as he walked down the hall. Each step sounded louder in the stillness, each creak like a warning. The old house seemed to hold its breath, listening, waiting. He reached the basement door, and as he opened it, a cold draft wafted up, carrying the sharp tang of damp earth and something worse – an edge of rot that tightened his grip on the railing. For a moment, he hesitated, but the whimper grew louder, tinged with a terror that clawed at his nerves.

Taking a steadying breath, Tom started down the stairs.

The descent felt endless, each step stretching longer than the last, as though he was moving deeper into some place where the familiar world faded. Shadows thickened around him, the air pressing in colder, heavier. He reached the bottom and paused, his eyes adjusting to the dim light. There, huddled in the corner, Bobby sat with his knees drawn to his chest, his small body shaking. He stared straight ahead, eyes locked on something unseen in the far corner.

"What's got you scared now?" Tom muttered, trying to keep his tone steady, but his hands were clammy, his pulse a drumbeat in his ears.

Bobby looked up, his face pale as chalk, his wide eyes glazed with fear. And then Tom saw it – the thin line of blood trickling down his brother's chin. A fresh bruise marked Bobby's cheek, dark and swollen, his lip split and raw. Tom's throat tightened as a chill crept down his spine.

"He is here," Bobby whispered, his voice barely audible, hoarse with terror. "Tom... he is here."

Tom's gaze shifted to the corner Bobby was staring at, but there was only darkness, shadows pooling thick and black, like ink spreading into the walls. The air grew colder, and Tom watched his own breath mist in front of him, lingering like a ghost.

"Quit it, Bobby. There's no one here but us," he said, his voice rough. But even as the words left his mouth, he couldn't shake the feeling that they weren't alone. The room felt heavy, something watching, something waiting, something ravenous.

Bobby shook his head, a tear slipping down his cheek. "He is here, Tom," he whispered, his voice almost gone. "He's always here."

Tom felt his skin prickle. He took a step closer to Bobby, and that's when he saw it – a flicker of movement in the corner. At first, he thought it was just a trick of the light, a shadow cast by the dim bulb. But then it shifted, coalescing into a form, an outline of something that seemed to breathe, its edges blurring in and out of the darkness.

And then he saw the face. Hollow eyes, glistening like black pits, a mouth stretched wide in a grimace, lips peeled back over teeth yellowed and sharp. The features twisted and melted, as if struggling to break free of the shadows, a grotesque version of a face he knew. Tom's heart lurched as recognition struck – it was his mother's face. But not as it had been in life. This was something else, something pulled from a nightmare, wearing her face like a mask.

Without a thought, Tom grabbed Bobby, pulling him up the stairs, his legs moving on pure instinct. He could hear the thing behind them, its soft shuffling, and then a whisper, a scratchy, brittle sound that scraped against his ears like broken glass. It muttered words he couldn't understand, words that clawed at his mind. The basement door slammed behind them, and he collapsed on the floor, holding Bobby as they gasped for breath.

From that night on, the Dalton house was never the same. His mother's eyes grew colder, her silences longer, and Bobby's fear deepened. The whispers from the basement became a nightly presence, a soft murmur that seeped through the walls, filling the house like a dark fog. Tom tried to brush it off; to convince himself it was just Bobby's overactive imagination. But deep down, he knew better.

Something had been disturbed in that house, something that would never let them go.

The nights that followed that first encounter in the basement dragged by, each one pressing a little more heavily on the Dalton house, like the slow creep of rot spreading beneath the surface. Tom could feel it – a thick, creeping silence that settled in every corner, heavy and inescapable, like damp air that wouldn't clear. He tried to go about his business, tried to ignore the change settling over the house, but Bobby's cries and whispers frayed his nerves, unravelling his patience one thread at a time. The boy barely ate, rarely spoke. His wide, nervous eyes had dulled, as though he were staring into a space that no one else could see.

And Ruth? Ruth Dalton drifted through the house like a phantom, her gaze unfocused, her face hollow, as if the life had been leached from her veins. She moved quietly, her footsteps almost imperceptible, her eyes clouded, like windows smeared with dust. She would stand at the kitchen sink, her hands submerged in soapy water, staring out the window at something beyond the fields, her expression blank, her lips parted as if she'd forgotten how to close them.

One night, well past midnight, Tom found her there, still staring out that same window, her hands resting in the cold, grimy water. The moonlight cast shadows across her face, hollowing out her cheeks, making her skin look almost waxen, unreal. She didn't blink, didn't turn when he entered the room; her gaze remained fixed on whatever lay beyond the fields, her lips cracked and still.

"Mum?" he said, his voice uncertain, wavering in the dark. A prickling chill crept over his skin, his heart hammering as he waited for her to respond.

She didn't move, didn't even acknowledge him. He took a step closer, close enough to see the fine lines etched deep into her face, her cracked lips parched, as if she hadn't had a drink in days. A chill settled over him, a feeling like he was peering over the edge of a cliff, staring into something vast and empty.

"Mum?" he tried again, louder this time, his voice shaking.

Slowly, she turned her head, her hollow gaze locking onto his. For a moment, something flickered there – recognition, fear, perhaps guilt. But it vanished as quickly as it had appeared, replaced by that same empty, distant stare.

"Tom..." she murmured, her voice low, rasping, as though she hadn't spoken in years. "Do not go down to the basement. Whatever you do... don't go down there." Her gaze drifted back to the window, her lips moving silently, forming words he couldn't hear.

The next morning, she was gone.

Tom woke to a house thick with the sickly scent of something foul, a stench that twisted his stomach. His hands shook as he tore through every room, flinging open cupboards and doors, but she was nowhere to be found. The odour clung to every surface, lingering like a terrible memory.

He found Bobby in the kitchen, sitting at the table with his knees pulled to his chest, his eyes bloodshot and staring. His face was drained, pale as milk, his gaze fixed on the basement door. Tom wanted to shake him, to demand answers, to scream that this was all his fault – but the words died in his throat. Bobby looked empty, as though something vital had been hollowed out, leaving only a shell.

"She's gone, Bobby," Tom said, his voice rough, barely more than a whisper.

Bobby didn't move, didn't even blink. "She is not gone," he murmured, his voice so faint it was barely a breath. "She is down there. I heard her last night... I heard her whispering."

A chill ran through Tom, prickling his skin as his eyes drifted to the basement door. The house was silent now, only the faint ticking of the clock filling the room, but he felt a presence, something lurking just beyond sight, watching.

Days turned into weeks, and whispers began in the town. The people of Fallen Ridge started talking, their voices hushed, their glances wary whenever they passed Tom in the street. They asked questions – questions he couldn't answer, questions he didn't want to answer. But as the days wore on, the whispers grew louder, the questions sharper, and Tom felt the walls closing in around him, the weight of his mother's disappearance pressing down on him like a stone.

He took to patrolling the town, his boots hitting the pavement in hard, deliberate strides, his gaze cold and unyielding. The townsfolk soon stopped asking. After all, Fallen Ridge was a place that kept its secrets buried deep, and Ruth Dalton was just one more ghost in a town haunted by many.

But Bobby couldn't move on. He grew quieter, more withdrawn, his gaze fixed on something beyond the visible, something that Tom couldn't see or understand. Hours passed with him sitting by the basement door, his eyes vacant, his lips moving as if in conversation with someone only he could hear.

The nights became torment, Bobby's soft, pitiful whimpering drifting through the house like a lullaby from hell. It started low, a barely audible whisper that slid under doors and through walls, filling every corner with dread so thick it choked the air. Tom lay awake, staring at the ceiling, listening to Bobby's voice, trembling and indistinct, muttering words he couldn't quite make out.

One night, unable to bear it any longer, he crept down the stairs, his footsteps silent against the old wooden boards, and stopped outside Bobby's door. He could hear his brother's voice, thin and cracked, the words slipping through the crack under the door like poison.

"She's here," Bobby whispered, his voice fractured. "She is down there... she is waiting."

A dark rage twisted in Tom's gut, a heat rising within him he couldn't control. He flung the door open, his eyes blazing as he stepped into the room. Bobby looked up, his face ashen, his wide eyes shimmering with terror.

"Enough!" Tom hissed, his voice low and venomous. "There is no one down there. Mum is gone. Do you hear me? She is gone."

Bobby's lip trembled, his gaze shifting to the shadows behind Tom, tears gathering in his eyes. "She is not gone, Tom," he whispered, his voice barely a breath. "She is always here."

For a moment, Tom felt a flicker of fear – a cold, insidious doubt that crept into his mind, winding through his thoughts like a snake. But he shoved it down, buried it beneath the anger churning inside him.

After that, Bobby grew silent, his voice fading, his eyes empty. And then, one night, he too disappeared.

Tom returned to an empty house, the air thick with the familiar stench of decay, the scent pressing in on him, heavy and unyielding. He searched every room, every cupboard, every shadowed corner, but there was no sign of Bobby. Only the silence remained, swallowing the house whole.

Years drifted by like spectres in the fog, each one bleeding into the next, hollowing Tom out bit by bit. He stayed in Fallen Ridge, tethered to the town by invisible chains, bound as surely as if the land itself held him captive. As he grew older, he transformed from a wiry, angry boy roaming the fields into a looming figure of quiet menace – a man who wore authority like armour, shielding him from the wounds of his past.

He took up the badge at twenty-two. Sheriff Boone, who'd served Fallen Ridge since the days when horses still clopped down Main Street, took one look at Tom and knew his own time had come. With a hand that trembled, the old man passed Tom the badge, his gaze flickering away, unable to meet Tom's eyes. No one questioned it. Boone was past his prime, and Tom? Tom was exactly what the Ridge needed – or, perhaps, exactly what it deserved.

The badge was cold and weighty on his chest, a gleaming silver star that caught the light like the edge of a blade. The power it brought... he wore that, too, like armour. Everyone in the Ridge knew better than to cross him, to challenge him. If you had a problem, you went to Sheriff Dalton, and he made it disappear. But nothing came for free, and in Fallen Ridge, no one dared ask the price.

Tom made his rounds through town, his boots heavy on the cracked pavement, his gaze sharp and unyielding. People glanced his way, eyes wary, faces pale, and glanced away. They felt his power, a chill that seeped through their skin, settling deep in their bones. Tom thrived on that fear, drank it down like a man dying of thirst. It was the only thing that kept the darkness at bay, the only thing that dulled the memories that clawed at him in the quiet.

Yet, no matter how much control he amassed, how many favours he collected, the darkness never truly left. It lingered at the edges of his mind, whispering in the dead of night. He saw it in the shadows filling his house, in the corners where the light refused to reach. Sometimes, late at night, he'd hear Bobby's voice – a faint, pitiful whimper slipping through the walls, filling the silence with a sorrow so profound it felt as though it could swallow him whole.

The people of Fallen Ridge had their theories. They whispered about the Dalton house, about the family that had vanished without a trace, leaving only Tom behind. Some claimed he'd killed them, buried them out in the fields where no one would ever find them. Others said they'd simply walked away, abandoning him. But no one dared ask him, not to his face. The badge gleamed cold and hard on his chest, a reminder that Sheriff Dalton was not a man to be questioned.

One winter's night, nearly a decade after he'd taken up the badge, Tom received a call. It was Old Man Grady, his voice crackling over the line, shaking as he spoke of noises – of something moving near the tree line by the Dalton place. Grady was a jittery old coot, half-blind and jumpy as a hare, but something in Tom's gut twisted, a pull he couldn't ignore. He grabbed his coat and torch and set off into the bitter cold.

The Dalton house loomed dark and silent, its windows like dead eyes staring into the night. The paint had peeled away long ago, leaving the wood bare, rotting in the damp air. Tom hadn't set foot inside in years, hadn't dared to face the shadows lingering within those walls. But tonight, something called to him. A whisper that slipped beneath his skin, filling him with a dread so profound it made his stomach twist.

He stood in the yard, his breath misting in the cold, his torch casting a narrow beam that barely cut through the darkness. The ground was frozen solid, and the trees stood bare, their branches clawing at the sky like twisted fingers.

And then he heard it – the soft, pitiful whimper that had haunted his dreams since childhood. The sound drifted through the night, frail and broken, like the cry of a child lost in the dark. It was Bobby's voice, unmistakable, calling to him from the depths of the house.

Tom's heart hammered against his ribs, his skin prickling as he took a step forward, his boots crunching over the frozen ground. The front door loomed before him, warped and swollen with age, but as he reached for the handle, it swung open on its own; the hinges creaking like a scream in the silence.

The darkness inside was thick, stifling, curling into every corner like smoke. He felt his pulse quicken as he stepped across the threshold, his torch casting faint, wavering beams over dust-covered walls and crumbling wood. There was a smell of rot and decay that curled in his gut, chilling him to the bone.

As he made his way down the hall, the whimpering grew louder, past his mother's old bedroom. The door was ajar, revealing a bed draped in dust, sheets brittle and grey. The walls seemed to pulse with each step he took, as if the house itself were alive, watching him.

He reached the basement door, feeling the cold seeping through it – a chill that cut straight to the bone. His hand trembled as he reached for the handle, pushing the door open slowly. The darkness within was absolute, swallowing his torch beam, but he could hear the voice now, close, almost tangible.

"Help me, Tom..." The words were faint, broken, barely more than a breath, but unmistakable.

He descended, each step creaking underfoot, the air thickening around him, as though he were sinking into a place where light and warmth held no meaning. The walls closed in, pressing against him, squeezing the air from his lungs.

At the bottom, he paused, his torch casting a weak, trembling light across the room. And there, huddled in the corner, was Bobby. His face was deathly pale, eyes wide and glassy with terror, his body trembling as he stared at something behind Tom.

A chill crawled down Tom's spine, the hairs at his nape standing on end. He turned slowly, his torch slicing through the shadows, but there was nothing there. Only darkness, impenetrable, swallowing every sliver of light.

"Tom... he is here..." Bobby's whisper was barely audible, his gaze fixed on something lurking just over Tom's shoulder.

Tom's heart skipped, cold fear coiling around him as he took a step back, his torch flickering, casting twisted shadows across the walls. And then, from the darkness, a face emerged—a face twisted and warped, staring back at him with hollow, sightless eyes. His mother's face, or what remained of it, peering from the shadows with a hunger, a rage that turned his blood to ice.

The torch slipped from his hand, clattering to the floor, its beam spinning wildly, casting eerie shapes across the room. He stumbled back, breath catching in his throat, every instinct urging him to run. But the face didn't move. It only stared, that empty gaze cutting through him, filling him with a terror so profound it felt as though his very soul were unravelling.

Then, as suddenly as it had appeared, the face vanished. The darkness closed in, thick, leaving only Bobby's faint, pitiful whimper echoing through the silence.

Tom staggered up the stairs, his hands shaking, his breath shallow and panicked. He stumbled out into the night, the cold air biting at his skin, his mind a whirl of terror. Even as he fled, he could still hear Bobby's voice, a faint whisper in the darkness, filling the night with an endless sorrow.

From that day forward, Sheriff Tom Dalton ruled the Ridge with an iron fist, a figure of quiet fury and dread, haunted by the ghosts of his past. The townsfolk knew better than to ask questions, to probe into the secrets he kept buried deep behind his cold, unyielding stare.

But every night, alone in his bed, he could still hear them – a faint, pitiful whisper sliding through the darkness, reminding him of what he had buried, of the darkness that would never let him go.

The years drifted by, casting a shadow over Sheriff Tom Dalton's life as he held Fallen Ridge in a quiet chokehold, his authority absolute yet tempered by a creeping darkness that only he could feel. On the surface, his power seemed unassailable; his word was law, and no one dared defy him. But beneath that iron facade lay a mind haunted, gnawed at by memories and whispers, a torment that festered unseen, like a wound left to rot.

People whispered about Tom – the stories, the rumours about the Dalton house, and the ghosts that clung to it – but always in hushed voices, their gazes flicking warily over their shoulders. They knew better than to cross him, sensed that his silence held the town's darkest secrets, secrets best left undisturbed.

Yet the darkness within him never truly quieted. It clawed at the edges of his sanity, whispering to him in the dead of night. Shadows flickered in the corners of his vision, movements that vanished the moment he turned to look. And sometimes, he'd see his mother's face, gaunt and ghostly, her hollow eyes filled with accusation, peering at him from the shadows of his bedroom.

And then there were the voices. Every night, he lay in bed, straining against the silence only to hear Bobby's thin, broken cries drifting through the dark, filling the air with a sorrow so deep it felt like it could pull him under. Tom tried to shut it out, burying it beneath the weight of his authority. But it was always there, gnawing at him, dragging him back into memories he couldn't escape.

One night, unable to bear it any longer, he rose, dressed, and left the house, stepping into the mist-shrouded streets. The air was thick with fog, curling around him like ghostly fingers, and the town lay silent, the streets empty, as if holding its breath. He walked with purpose, his footsteps echoing in the stillness, his mind a storm of memories and regrets.

The Dalton house loomed before him, dark and silent, its windows empty and unseeing, like eyes that had forgotten how to live. He stood on the porch, hand hovering over the doorknob, his heart pounding. For a moment, a flicker of fear twisted in his gut, a chill that crawled up his spine. But he pushed it aside, gritted his teeth, and turned the handle.

The suffocating darkness closed in, thick and cold. The air hung heavy with the faint odour of decay, clinging to every surface, curling into his lungs with each shallow breath. He moved down the hall, past rooms filled with shadows that seemed to stretch and breathe, following him like silent watchers. And then he stopped, his gaze locked on the basement door.

It loomed before him, closed tight, but he could feel the chill seeping through, a cold that made his bones ache. Slowly, his hand trembling, he reached for the handle and pushed it open.

The blackness beyond swallowed the torch beam, rendering it weak. But he could hear them now – the voices, close and clear.

"Tom..." Bobby's voice, fragile and broken, drifted up from the shadows. "Tom... please..."

The hairs on the back of his neck prickled, his pulse quickening as he stepped onto the stairs. Each creak underfoot felt like a heartbeat, echoing his own dread. The walls seemed to close in as he descended, pressing the air from his lungs, the darkness growing heavier, deeper.

At the bottom, he paused, his torch casting a feeble glow across the room. And then he saw them.

Bobby was there, huddled in the corner, his face pale as moonlight, eyes wide with terror. His skin seemed translucent, ghostly; his gaze locked onto something in the shadows just behind Tom.

Then came the sound – a soft, shuffling movement, like fabric brushing against the walls. He turned slowly, heart thudding, breath tight, catching in his throat.

Out of the darkness, a face emerged – a face twisted and hollow, staring at him with empty, accusing eyes. His mother. Her gaze burned into him, filled with a hunger, a fury he could feel tearing into his soul.

"Tom..." she whispered, her voice thin and jagged, barely more than a breath. "You left us... you left me..."

He stumbled back, his mind reeling, hands shaking. "No... you're gone. You're *dead!*" he cried, his voice raw, filled with desperation.

But she kept advancing, her face contorted, her eyes hollow yet piercing, filled with a sorrow that cut through him, sharp and relentless. Behind her, Bobby's small face stared up at him, pale and drawn, filled with a terror that mirrored his own.

Tom felt his knees weaken, his mind unravelling as the voices swirled around him, accusing, whispering, dragging him deeper into the shadows of his own guilt, his own fear.

"Tom..." his mother's voice came, cold and empty, filling the air. "You cannot escape us. You cannot bury the past."

He closed his eyes, his body trembling, mind flooded with memories, things he had tried so hard to bury. The darkness pressed closer, smothering him, pulling him into its depths.

When he opened his eyes, he was alone. The basement lay silent, empty, the air thick with dust and decay. But their faces, their voices, lingered, filling the silence with a sorrow that was endless, unyielding.

He staggered up the stairs, mind clouded, heart pounding, and stumbled out into the chilly night. Mist curled around him, biting and frigid, but even in the quiet, he could still hear them, faint voices whispering through the darkness, filling the air with a sorrow that would never let him go.

From that night forward, Sheriff Tom Dalton was a broken man, his authority a shadow of the fear and sorrow that haunted him. Fallen Ridge kept its distance, and no one dared ask about the secrets he held, the ghosts that tormented him. But on still nights, if you stood near the Dalton house, you could hear them – the voices, soft and sorrowful, drifting through the darkness, a reminder of the past that Sheriff Dalton would never escape, the ghosts that would haunt him forever.

EPILOGUE

THE ROAD OUT OF the Ridge is long and winding, cloaked in a stillness that feels almost unnatural. Travellers who leave often remark on how the air feels lighter beyond the valley, as if they've slipped free from some invisible weight. Yet, for those who remain – and there are many – there's an unnameable pull that binds them to this place, something they feel with every heavy step, an ache in their bones that whispers of roots they cannot see. The Ridge claims its own, etching itself into their marrow, as inescapable as breath.

Sheriff Dalton's house stands empty now, its windows dark and hollow, yet some swear they've glimpsed a figure on the porch, face hidden in shadow, pacing as though awaiting a visitor who never arrives. Just beyond, the grocery store lies in quiet disuse, and though Daisy's register collects dust, her perfume lingers – a faint, ghostly reminder, like a memory tinged with decay. They say that if you listen closely at night, you might hear a child's whimper, the faintest echo drifting through the aisles before silence folds in again.

Further along, the church slumbers beneath a delicate film of dust. Pastor Lou's Bible lies open on the pulpit, its pages untouched, their edges yellowed with age. The townsfolk avoid the church, shunning its shadowed interior, muttering of a coldness that seeps from its walls, as though some presence within has drawn out the warmth. Those who pass by the house have reported glimpsing a woman's shadow at the altar – a pale face, empty eyes, mouth frozen in an unending scream.

Then there is widow Larkin's house, where silence reigns as resolutely as she once did. They say her mirrors still hold her image alongside those of her husbands, faces twisted with something far darker than grief. The windows are boarded, yet some swear they have seen Margaret and her three husbands behind the glass, her eyes sharp and unyielding, fierce as ever, peering out through the decay.

New faces occasionally come to Fallen Ridge, some drawn by choice, others by a pull they cannot name, lured by an unseen force that lies thick in the valley air. They call it the town's charm – a quiet solitude that invites introspection. But Fallen Ridge is not silent; it has never truly been silent. It murmurs, its voice a soft hum that settles in the back of one's mind and deepens with each day, sinking roots into the soul.

Some say the town collects its secrets, stores them as one might press delicate moths between the pages of an ancient book, preserved but hidden from view. And when the night comes, when the town falls utterly still, those secrets stir, voices spilling from empty rooms, winding through deserted streets, lingering in mirrors and wells and shadows that no one dares to enter. They murmur of lives concealed, of sins soaked into the earth, stories that cling and remain.

Because Fallen Ridge does not let go.

If ever you find yourself in Fallen Ridge, beware the silence. Listen to the faint rustle of leaves, the creak of doors that have long stood closed. They carry the voices of those who once tried to leave, who thought they might escape. But no one truly escapes. The Ridge holds its own close.

And if, one day, you feel a chill creep along your spine, if a whisper in the wind knows your name, then you too have been claimed.

Fallen Ridge is a place for secrets. And once it holds yours, it never releases them.

About the Author

RJ Derby grew up with a fascination for the unseen and the unknown, often found devouring ghost stories by flashlight and scrawling down spine-chilling tales of his own. A native of a small town in Western Australia, RJ Derby has always been drawn to the eerie side of small-town life – the secrets that lurk behind closed doors, the stories whispered on dark, empty streets, and the shadows cast by every family's history.

Fallen Ridge is RJ's latest exploration into the world of psychological horror. Inspired by a lifelong fascination with haunted places and the mysteries of human nature, he has woven a story that invites readers to peer into the depths of fear and guilt, to see what lies beyond the safety of daylight.

When not writing, the author can be found hiking through old forests, browsing used bookstores for forgotten ghost stories, or savouring late-night horror movies. He currently resides in Merredin, Western Australia, where he's at work on his next novel, promising readers even more thrills, chills, and late-night reading with the lights on.